A CHRISTMAS TO DIE FOR

A WONDERLAND BOOKS COZY MYSTERY
BOOK FOUR

M.P. BLACK

For my family—you make Christmas cozy.

CHAPTER 1

*W*onderland Books—which looked like a miniature log-cabin—measured about 400 square feet, and so it was a tight squeeze to host so many people for the Clyde Digby book reading. The author himself sat on a tall stool at the opposite end from the small counter, right under a sprig of mistletoe.

From behind the counter, Alice Hartford worried. She worried that the audience, most of them standing and pressed against each other or a bookshelf, were uncomfortable. She worried the bestselling Digby was unhappy reading to such a small audience. And looking at her watch, she worried the event would run out of time and it would delay the next reading—the children's story hour with Santa Claus.

"Calm down," her friend Ona Rodriguez said. The eyepatch she wore over one eye glittered with rhinestones. "Everyone's loving this. Clyde Digby's great. And there's plenty of time before the story hour for the kids starts."

"But no sign of Santa yet."

"There's still time. Relax. Focus on Digby's reading instead—he's amazing."

Alice let out a long sigh. Maybe Ona was right. She ought to enjoy this. The bookstore looked festive, with ornaments hanging from bookshelves and from the log-cabin beams above. A bonsai tree, cut and decorated like a miniature Christmas tree, stood on her counter. And near the door, a mannequin in a Santa costume welcomed visitors. It had a bag of treats around its neck and a small sign that said, "Ho! Ho! Ho! Grab a candy cane!"

She pushed aside the dozen to-do's fluttering around in her head and focused on Clyde Digby.

The fifty-ish author—a balding, cardigan-wearing man with a giant, graying beard—was reading from his latest book, a novella called "The Mistletoe Scandal." Alice had a stack of the thin paperbacks in her bookstore, including on the counter. Ahead of the reading, she'd sold more copies of this one book than any other this year.

The cover was enticing: It showed a hunky, bare-chested guy kissing a woman on her neck under a sprig of mistletoe. The woman, head thrown back, was in a state of ecstasy.

The cover had another thing in its favor: A sticker announced the author would donate his proceeds from book sales to a charity.

From his perch on the stool, Digby read:

"He gestured at something above her head.

'Mistletoe again,' he said.

'Miles, this time...'

'Yes?'

'Kiss me.'

And he did. He kissed her with an intensity that she'd longed for—that she now understood she needed more than anything—and her body burned with what felt like a lifetime of pent-up passion."

The audience held its breath. As Digby continued his reading, the bookstore was so silent Alice could hear the crunch of boots on the snow outside.

Convincing Digby to do a reading at Blithedale's tiny bookstore had been a major coup. He was a bestselling romance author with a home in the Blithedale Woods (and another in Costa Rica, plus an apartment in New York City). For most of his career, he'd published under pseudonyms—Jessica Spence, Leigh Lowry, Madeleine Darcy—but in recent years, he'd switched to his own name. His readers didn't mind; his sales had only increased. Alice hadn't read his novels, which ranged from sweet contemporary to spicy Regency romances, but Ona had.

A stack of Ona's Clyde Digby paperbacks, including a few under pseudonyms, sat on the counter. She'd taken a break from work at her hotel—the Pemberley Inn—hoping Digby would sign them all.

Digby reached the end of his reading and the audience let out a collective sigh. Then people clapped. The first eager fans rushed forward to get their books signed. Shoes shuffled, heavy winter overcoats rustled, and chatter filled Wonderland Books.

"Wow," Ona said.

"As good as you'd expected?" Alice asked.

"Better. I'm going to get in line."

Ona grabbed her stack of books and headed for the throng of people gathered at the other end near Digby.

Meanwhile, Alice got busy helping customers. A woman from out of town bought a stack of books, including Digby's novella and *A Christmas Carol* by Charles Dickens. She spoke of getting into the Christmas spirit, and as Alice rang up her purchases, she told the customer about the Blithedale Christmas Fair.

"I saw an ad for it online," the woman said. "Sounds wonderful. Is it a tradition?"

Alice nodded. "But I'm told it was modest in past years. We've expanded it a lot. We're going to have a parade with horse carriages, and if you walk a little way down Main Street, you'll see the fairgrounds with rows and rows of stalls. Vendors are selling crafts and clothes and food."

"Oh, I'll have to check it out. And I'll come back with my husband and kids, too." She took her bag of books from Alice. "I came for Digby's reading and didn't know what to expect. I'm surprised at how quaint this town is. Blithedale has a shady reputation, doesn't it? I mean, there's been several murders."

Another customer in line spoke up. He said, "Yeah, I read about the murders, too. And I actually came to town years ago and visited the bookstore—" He looked around. "—but it looked different back then. And the owner was so rude, I left."

"His name is Bunce," Alice muttered.

"Is he your boss?"

"He's not my boss," Alice said emphatically, annoyed that he'd assume Bunce—Bunce, of all people—was her boss. Then, aware that she'd snapped at the customer, she softened her tone. "This is my business. This is my bookstore. The old Blithedale Books is gone."

In fact, Blithedale Books was originally owned by Alice's mom. But when her mom got cancer, she sold to Bunce, and 9-year-old Alice and her mom moved from Blithedale. When Alice returned earlier this year—20 years after she'd left, 20 years after her mom had died—she discovered a run-down Blithedale Books, neglected by a bitter, mean old Bunce. Eventually, bulldozers tore down the old bookstore and Alice established a new one, Wonderland Books.

She took a deep breath and let it out. The old bookstore

and Bunce were both gone. Soon, people would forget about the cantankerous bookseller and his shabby store. Time would obscure the past. She hoped they would forget about the recent murders, too, and instead think of Blithedale as the best place in the world to celebrate Christmas.

Alice and her friends, Ona and Becca, had drawn on their own business reserves to invest in this year's Christmas Fair. Plus, the Blithedale Future Fund—a community investment fund run by the three of them to revitalize businesses in town—had contributed a lot to the budget. Everyone was counting on the Christmas fair being a success.

And if it isn't...? If no one shows up...?

Everyone was counting on the event to draw big crowds and increase revenue for the town.

As part of Blithedale's ongoing efforts to revitalize, Mayor Townsend had invested heavily in this year's fair. A demolition contractor had torn down an abandoned office building to make space for the fairgrounds. An event production company had been contracted to develop holiday parade floats. They also provided horse carriages and horses to pull the floats, stalls, porta-potties, and sound systems—plus a generator to run it all.

To pay for everything, the Blithedale Municipality had taken a short-term loan from the Tilbury Savings and Loans Bank. It would need to be repaid at the beginning of next year. If the fair failed, the town—heavily indebted—would face serious financial problems. And by extension, so would local businesses like her bookstore. They were all betting a lot on this event.

As another customer brought a pile of books to the counter, she pushed the negative thoughts aside. People were buying books. And she told each out-of-towner about the fair, hoping they'd come back or tell their friends. Ideally both.

We're all doing what we can.

As the romance fans shuffled out, parents with children wandered into Wonderland Books. Alice checked her watch again. The organizers of the fair had assigned a Santa Claus to come for the story hour. He should've arrived by now.

She grabbed her phone and dialed the number for Ben Ridgeway, who was involved in staffing the fair. Resting her phone under her cheek, so she could have her hands free, she gift wrapped books for a customer: hardbound editions of *The Adventure of the Blue Carbuncle* by Arthur Conan Doyle and *Hercule Poirot's Christmas* by Agatha Christie.

"Hi, Ben—the Santa Claus I ordered, well, he's not here..."

Ben asked her to hold while he checked.

"Alice, sorry about this. Vickers, who's in charge of the Santa contest and the Santas, he says the guy should arrive any moment now."

She hung up and tended to the next customer, who was buying more Clyde Digby books. Then Ona returned with her pile of signed books, a big grin on her face.

"It's like Christmas came early," she said. "Who doesn't love a pile of books?"

A man in a Santa costume shambled into the bookstore, and Alice thought, *Finally, now we can get the kids' story hour started.*

But when he turned toward her and scowled, she froze. Despite the fake Santa beard, she recognized his pasty face at once. Her heart did a backflip.

"Bunce?"

"Books," he grumbled, looking around at the bookstore with disdain. "I hate books."

CHAPTER 2

"*S*anta!" a little girl squeaked with joy. She grabbed a fistful of Bunce's red pants and tugged happily.

Bunce scowled down at her. He muttered, "Hands off, you little rat," and shook himself free. Then turned to Alice. "Let's get this over with."

Alice had a clear vision of the future: children crying, parents offended, customers never coming back. And what would people say about Blithedale's Christmas fair if this was the kind of Santa they met?

Someone's got to do something.

She knew who that someone was.

"No, thank you," she said.

She grabbed Bunce by the shoulders, and as he protested —"What do you think you're doing?!"—she turned him around and marched him out of Wonderland Books. She gave him a little shove, so he stumbled out onto the sidewalk.

"Go back to Florida," Alice said.

"I'm your Santa," Bunce grumbled, "whether you like it or not. They're not sending another."

"Then I'll find my own Santa."

7

Alice turned on her heels and strode back into her bookstore.

"Well done," Ona said, clearly impressed. Then she frowned. "But now what do we do?"

The bookstore was filling up with kids, many of them already sitting on the floor in anticipation of story hour, hemming in Clyde Digby, who was stuck talking to a couple of diehard fans. More parents were arriving by the second. Soon, Wonderland Books would reach maximum capacity.

Alice thought of who she could enlist as Santa Claus for story hour.

"Ona…"

"Sorry, sweetie. I'll do Jane Austen impersonations, but I don't do Santa."

"Then who—?"

"Becca's too busy at the diner. Beau's got a show going on later today at the theater. Mayor MacDonald is working at the fair, getting things ready for the first parade. What about Chief Jimbo?"

Blithedale's young chief of police was the town's only cop. Alice didn't have a high opinion of him, but despite his failure to investigate recent murders, Mayor MacDonald insisted Jimbo was learning and getting better. Alice couldn't decide whether to feel frustrated or sorry for Jimbo. Usually, she felt both.

She shook her head. "Jimbo has stage fright. He told me so himself. He'd panic if he had to face an audience of kids."

"I'm out of ideas," Ona said.

"Me, too."

Alice looked around the bookstore at the waiting kids and parents, and she bit her lip. She didn't recognize most of the families. Which ought to be a good thing. It meant they'd driven all the way from Tilbury Town or came from even farther away. But if story hour turned out to be a fiasco, would any of them ever come back? And what would they tell their friends and relatives—"Stay away from Blithedale, it's a bust"?

This whole thing could be a disaster.

A little boy approached Clyde Digby, interrupting the romance fans.

"If you're Santa," he asked with a critical frown, "where's your hat?"

Digby smiled, clearly amused. "I must've left it in my sleigh, along with my presents."

"My momma says you're gonna read a book."

"Oh, does she?"

Alice had an idea. She didn't let herself think too much about it, knowing she'd lose her nerve if she did. Instead, she hurried over to the mannequin, pulled off the hat and coat, and strode to the back of the store.

She held out the Santa costume to Digby, and he raised both eyebrows in surprise. The look she gave him, she hoped, made it clear that she was asking for his help. No, begging for his help. She even mouthed the word, *Please.*

He gazed at her. She couldn't tell if he was amused or annoyed—his face hid whatever emotions moved within him. He'd make an excellent poker player if he wasn't one already.

Finally, he nodded and took the costume from her. He unbuttoned his cardigan and slipped on the Santa coat, then the hat.

Turning to face the children, he spoke in a deep and resonant voice: "Ho, ho, ho. Who would like to hear a Christmas story?"

"Yay!" the kids cried out.

He reached for the nearest book display, picking up *How the Grinch Stole Christmas!,* and turned to the first page.

Alice backed away, her heart racing. She would find a way

to thank him. She only hoped this didn't scare him off and he'd never come back to Wonderland Books again.

She returned to the counter. Ona gave her a high five.

"Phew," Alice said. "That was close. But, Ona, what the heck's going on—why is Bunce back in town?"

"Must be for the Santa contest."

"He came out of retirement and traveled all the way up from Florida, simply to play Santa? That seems crazy. And pointless, too. I mean, who would ever vote for Bunce as the best Santa?"

"Well, actually, last year he won."

"He what!?"

Several parents turned and frowned at Alice.

She dropped her voice. "He won the Santa contest?"

"It came as a surprise, but they recounted the votes, and he won it fair and square. I bet he's hoping to win again. There's a big cash prize."

Alice couldn't make sense of it. Bunce was the last person on the planet who'd make a suitable Santa. But the part that did make sense was the cash prize—that would attract Bunce.

She watched Clyde Digby for a while. He seemed to be enjoying himself, and he was a wonderful reader. The kids made sounds—ooh's and aah's and gasps—when the Grinch stole everyone's presents. One little kid shot to her feet and exclaimed indignantly, "You can't do that. You can't steal presents."

Her parents gently coaxed her down onto the floor again.

As the reading went on, Alice's attention drifted to the outside. The front door stood open, letting in cold air. Outside, a man in a Santa costume rushed down the sidewalk.

Her stomach tightened. Bunce?

No, it wasn't Bunce. This man had a leaner figure.

He was hurrying down Main Street, dodging other pedestrians, as he clutched a leather document pouch under one arm. Professionals—her association was with bankers or business consultants—would keep notepads or files or even a laptop in a leather pouch like that.

"Looks like an architect late for a meeting," Ona remarked. "If that architect was wearing a Santa costume."

"He sure is in a hurry."

The Santa vanished from sight, just as a tall, gangly man ducked under the doorway and stepped inside. It was Todd Townsend, owner of *The Blithedale Record*, the local news site.

"All this Christmas cheer is bad for business," he said. "Nobody wants happy headlines."

"Oh, I don't know about that," Alice said. "I think people prefer their local news to be positive."

"Fun, maybe. But once it gets sentimental, people stop reading. Now, what people really want to read about is murder. And if it isn't murder, they want—"

He stopped himself. His eyes went wide. Then a grin spread across his face.

"As I was saying, if they don't want murder, they want sex." He gestured toward Clyde Digby. "And this is perfect. I can see the headline now: 'Spicy Santa Inspires a New Generation of Romance Readers.'"

Alice groaned. "Please, Todd—"

But Todd was already moving along the bookshelves, sneaking closer to the front, no doubt so he could corner Clyde Digby at the end of the reading. He dug out his phone and started snapping photos.

Alice buried her face in her hands.

CHAPTER 3

*I*n the afternoon, Alice closed the bookstore and joined her friends Ona and Becca—and the rest of Blithedale—at the Christmas fair.

The "Christmas village" stood in an empty lot, where Townsend Development's offices had recently been demolished. It was now packed with rows of vendor stalls. The aisles between the stalls led to an open area in front of a large stage with a giant Christmas tree in the middle.

In an hour, the fair's opening ceremony would begin. Alice wanted to check out the vendors and their wares before they headed for the main stage. Plus, she hoped to see Bunce again.

"Isn't seeing him once enough?" Becca asked, shaking her head. Becca Frye, a broad-shouldered woman with a curly mane of black hair, owned the What the Dickens Diner, the heart of Blithedale's social life. "I can't believe he's back. And I can't believe you got Clyde Digby to play Santa instead." She laughed. "No wonder Todd got so excited."

Ona smiled. "Did you see the story on *The Blithedale Record's* site?"

"He wrote that Digby made the parents hot and bothered, and then warmed the hearts of their children," Alice said, wincing at the memory of the news article. "He made it sound like Digby did a mash-up of the Grinch and a spicy romance. What if it's bad for business?"

"Oh, it'll be fine," Ona said. "Clyde Digby fans around the country will read it and think he's a saint."

Becca nodded. "And some of them may even jump in the car and head to Blithedale, hoping to spot their favorite author at the Christmas fair."

"I guess so..." Alice said. "But first Bunce and then—"

"Relax, Alice."

But as they wandered past the vendor stalls at the fair, she couldn't shake the feeling that Bunce's presence was a bad omen.

He cursed Mom's bookstore.

Well, maybe that was a little dramatic. At least she could confidently say he'd run it into the ground. And even if he wasn't a bad omen, he was bad business—and certainly *bad for business.*

With so much riding on the success of the fair, the last thing Blithedale needs is a guy who's bad for business.

Ona linked arms with her. "Come on, Alice. Cheer up. 'Tis the season to be jolly."

At that moment, they came to a stall run by Esther Lucas. Esther ran Love Again, the town's consignment store. Her stall featured winter clothes, including beautiful knit sweaters with reindeer and pine-tree designs. She also sold hand-knit teddy bears with Santa hats. Some even had little bow ties on. They were so cute and soft and cuddly, Alice was tempted to buy one for herself.

"These aren't consignment items, are they?" she asked.

"No, I made the sweaters and the teddies," Esther said. "I work on them throughout the year, so I have lots. But I

13

honestly don't know if I'll have enough this year. Look." She gestured out at the crowd. "The fair hasn't officially kicked off yet, and it's already getting crowded."

Alice scanned the crowd. And there, moving among the people, was a man in a Santa costume.

Bunce?

She excused herself, put the teddy back, and dodged through the crowd, nearly colliding with a man whose attention was on a cone full of roasted nuts.

But when she caught up with the Santa, she saw that under the fake beard he was a young guy. He was crouched down by a little girl, smiling, and asking what presents she wanted for Christmas.

"Hey, Alice," someone said, and she turned around.

Andrea Connor stood in the nearest stall, waving at her to come over.

"Want to try my new cranberry pie?"

Andrea ran Bonsai & Pie, a cafe selling, as the name suggested, bonsai trees and all kinds of pies. Her stall featured bonsai trees decked out as Christmas trees (like the one Alice had bought for Wonderland Books). Andrea served a sample of her cranberry pie and watched with anticipation as Alice speared the piece with a fork.

Generously dusted with powdered sugar, the pie looked like a winter landscape. Alice took a bite. The crust crunched and crumbled in her mouth, while the tartness of the cranberry hit the front of her tongue and then eased into a sweet aftertaste.

"Heavenly," she told Andrea. "As usual."

She looked over her shoulder, distracted for a moment by another man in a Santa outfit sauntering past her.

Andrea said, "Your mind is elsewhere, I can tell."

"I'm looking for someone in a Santa outfit."

She briefly explained what had happened at the bookstore, and Andrea sighed.

"Oh, I wish that man would stay away. But, Alice, finding him at the fair is like looking for a needle in a haystack."

Alice shrugged. "I'll keep my eyes peeled."

Bunce is easily recognizable, she thought. *How hard can it be?*

She caught sight of Becca and Ona up ahead, moving down the row of stalls toward the open space by the Christmas tree and main stage. She said goodbye to Andrea and zigzagged through the crowd, catching up with her friends as they came to the last stall.

"There you are," Becca said. "We thought we'd lost you. Look how many people there are."

Alice stared. She knew she must be gaping. But she really was amazed. The open space in front of the stage was no longer open. People milled back and forth, moving from one end to the other. Others stood in clusters near the Christmas tree at the center, drinking warm drinks and talking, no doubt waiting for the show to start.

There were people from Blithedale as well as out-of-towners, and among them, men and women in red hats and coats and big white beards. Talking to kids. Weaving in and out of the crowds. One was leaning against a stall, drinking hot chocolate and munching a donut. Another was on his phone talking to someone on a video call and laughing.

The fair didn't just feature a few Santas, but dozens of them.

Andrea had been right. Finding Bunce would be like looking for a needle in a haystack.

"That's a lot of Santas…" she mumbled.

Ona said, "Yeah, nothing like a big cash prize to attract lots of do-gooders, eh?"

"Don't be so cynical," Becca said. "A lot of these Santas put smiles on kids' faces. They're here because they love the job itself. Besides, only one of them will be crowned Santa of the Year—they can't count on winning the prize."

Ona saw a nearby stall she wanted to check out. As they headed toward it, Alice couldn't help but scan the Santas. They were men and women of all complexions, skinny and round, dark and fair, with smooth or gruff voices, and yet not one of them was Bunce.

The stall Ona wanted to check out bore a hand-carved wooden sign: "Mystic Tree Readings & Remedies." An incense stick in a stand burned, its fragrant smoke wafting out of the stall. The logo, a many-branched tree, looked familiar to Alice. She'd seen it outside the new-age store toward the end of Main Street. Alice had never visited the store, but Ona knew the owner, a young woman with long, black curls. She introduced herself as Kendra Digby.

"Digby?" Alice asked. "As in Clyde Digby?"

Kendra smiled. "Yes, he's my dad."

Ona added, "And Abigail Digby is Kendra's mom."

"Oh, of course."

Abigail Digby was hosting the Christmas fair. Alice had seen her name on countless documents that she, Ona, and Becca had reviewed. As managers of the Blithedale Future Fund, and investors in the Christmas fair, they'd poured over a lot of documents related to the fair—and Alice recalled the honorarium paid to Abigail Digby, a rather hefty fee considering that almost everyone involved was volunteering their time.

Abigail was the closest Blithedale came to having a socialite––and the one time Alice had met her, Abigail had been wearing fashionable designer wear—a Ferragamo coat, Prada shoes, a Gucci bag, Cartier jewelry—and shamelessly name-dropped the brands. Which stood out in Blithedale, where most people wore flannel shirts and jeans.

So it was surprising to see the daughter, Kendra, wearing

an old army jacket with colorful sewn-on patches showing chakra symbols.

Kendra sold crystals, tarot cards, incense, new age books and pamphlets, scented candles, herbal and medicinal teas, CDs with healing sounds, jewelry, pendulums, soaps, ritual oils, even pouches of herbs and spices. A sign on the counter advertised "Personal Tarot Readings."

Ona bought a bag of loose-leaf tea.

"I love this calming bedtime tea."

She opened the little bag, and Alice and Becca gave it a sniff. The scent of flowers and chamomile filled Alice's nose, along with something else—a hint of anise? If the tea was anything like it smelled, she could see why Ona liked it.

A woman passed them, the smell of her spiced apple cider competing with Kendra's incense and teas. From somewhere nearby, the smell of popcorn drifted across the crowd. Alice caught a whiff of fresh donuts.

Alice looked around, amazed at how many foods and clothes and toys and trinkets were on sale in the many stalls.

As she was gazing around, she caught sight of a man in red—a Santa—slipping between two stalls across the way from where she stood. Another Santa pursued him, squeezing between the stalls and catching him by the arm.

Could one of them be Bunce?

They struggled—and then the first Santa tore himself free. They were too far away for her to see their faces clearly. And all around her, the sound of talking and Christmas music drowned out what the Santas said. They disappeared down the gap between the stalls.

She stepped away from Kendra's stall, where Ona and Becca were busy examining the many things for sale, and she hurried after the two Santas.

Of the two stalls they'd slipped between, one was a cookie vendor and the other sold hand-crafted ornaments. Alice could see the Santas down the narrow gap between the stalls. If she followed them down this narrow alley, they would see her. So instead, she chose the passage on the other side of the ornament stall.

Slipping down the passage, she stopped at the end when she heard voices.

The two Santas stood in the space between the backs of the stalls and a fence. She couldn't see them and didn't want to risk a look in case they spotted her. But she could hear them clearly now. Both were men. One sounded nervous, the other gruff. Neither was Bunce, but before she could turn away, Alice was caught by what they said.

The nervous one said, "I know, I know, Wade, and I promise—"

"Your promises mean nothing," the gruff one said. "You've had time. You've had plenty of time."

"I'll get the money. I will."

"If you don't, you know what will happen."

The nervous one muttered something unintelligible.

The gruff one, Wade, said, "Tomorrow, Lewis. I want the money tomorrow. Or else."

"Tomorrow? I can't get you—"

Someone grunted and the chain-link fence rattled.

"Tomorrow," Wade repeated.

Alice heard footsteps. She took a chance and peeked around the corner of the stall. The one named Wade, his back to her, was striding away in the other direction. The remaining one, Lewis, leaned against the fence, his face in his hands.

Wade must have shoved Lewis against the fence.

A little taste of what's to come? she wondered.

Down the way, Wade turned into another passage between stalls, and in that instant, she recognized him by the leather pouch he carried under his arm. He was the Santa she'd seen rushing down Main Street earlier in the day.

What was this about money? And if Lewis didn't pay on time, how did Wade plan to carry out his threat? Was he threatening Lewis with violence? Could this even be a prelude to murder?

Alice shook her head.

You're getting paranoid, she chided herself as she turned to leave. *Every conflict doesn't end in murder.*

CHAPTER 4

$\mathcal{T}$he chain-link fence—the one Wade had shoved Lewis against—ringed the Christmas fair, running behind the stalls and stopping at the stage. A gate next to the stage said, "Staff & Volunteers Only."

Becca led Alice and Ona to the gate.

A familiar uniformed figure waved at them as they approached. It was Chief Jimbo, Blithedale's chief of police. He was a young guy with round, well-fed cheeks that gave the impression he hadn't lost all his baby fat yet. He looked too young for the job. His inexperience and fear of hard police work only reinforced this impression.

Before he could say anything, he sneezed. He buried his nose in a handkerchief and blew it with trumpet-like energy. His eyes were bloodshot, his face pale.

"Maybe you should be in bed," Becca said.

"Just a gold," he said, his stuffy nose making his voice nasal. "If I'm in bed, who's gonna do seguridy?"

"Oh, I think Blithedale will be all right for a day or two."

Alice suppressed a smile. Becca knew, as did everyone in town, that Chief Jimbo wasn't much of a lawman. He'd inherited the position from his dad, who'd been a respected chief of police. Maybe it was because of the dad's reputation —or simply goodwill toward the young cop—that Mayor MacDonald continued to keep Jimbo employed. Even after bungling so many investigations.

"I gan't let you go ingside," Chief Jimbo said, gesturing at the gate. "Staff only."

"We've got passes," Becca said, showing her pass. Alice and Ona brought out their passes, too. As funders of the fair, they had VIP access.

Chief Jimbo nodded and opened the gate for them. "Go ahead."

Alice, Becca, and Ona passed through the gate and into the staff-only area.

Inside the gate, a set of stairs to the left rose to the stage. Beyond that, two rows of trailers faced each other, a path of trampled snow separating them. At the end of that path stood a cluster of parade floats. Massive papier-mâché sculptures and other decorations rose from wagons, the nearest figure a giant reindeer with a bright red nose. And beyond that rose the ubiquitous wall of trees. In Blithedale, everywhere you looked, you saw trees.

A man on a ladder was working on the float behind the reindeer—a giant elf in a green, tasseled hat—apparently repairing an arm.

A group of people stood by one of the trailers. Not just any group, either. They were all men and women in Santa costumes. They were drinking from cups that sent wisps of steam trailing off in the cold air. Most had removed their fake beards, though a few boasted genuine facial hair. Alice studied their faces, unable to resist the urge to look for Bunce. But he wasn't among them.

Across from the Santas stood a trailer marked "Management & Logistics." A young man came out of the open door, a red scarf flung around his neck. It was Ben Ridgeway, who Alice had met at meetings to plan the fair.

He bounded down the steps and greeted them with a smile.

"Come to see how the sausage is made?"

"I don't know about sausage," Ona said. "But we're taking a look around before the show begins."

"It's going to be a hell of a show."

Alice said, "Ben, you're in charge of staffing. You sent me a volunteer Santa—Bunce—to do a book reading. Any idea where he is?"

Ben shook his head. "As you can see, we have a lot of Santas. It's very popular. Besides, Vickers is in charge of all Santa-related stuff."

"Ben," a woman said, standing in the trailer door. "Do you have the latest staffing schedule?"

Ben turned around. "I shared the file with you, Mom, and printed it out. It's the one on the cork board." Then he turned to Alice, Becca, and Ona and said, "You've all met my mom, right?"

He turned back to present her, but she'd ducked back inside the trailer.

"Oh," he said, sounding disappointed. "Next time."

"That's all right," Becca said. "We met Mariella at a budget meeting. Besides, you must be busy—we won't keep you."

The man Alice had seen on the ladder by the elf float jogged over to Ben. He had a full black beard and spoke with a Middle Eastern accent.

"Mr. Ridgeway," he said.

"Please, Mohammad, I've told you. Call me Ben."

The man nodded, a look of concern on his face. "Yes, Mr. —Ben. It's the elf. The arm falls off. I fixed it. But then it falls off again. It's the stitching."

"Let me take a look." Ben smiled at Alice and her friends. "Enjoy your tour."

As he walked away, Alice noticed that both he and Mohammad wore light-blue jackets that said "Ridgeway Cleaning" on the back. By now, she knew the company well. It was the biggest sponsor of the event. Mariella Ridgeway, its owner, had offered to provide staff and funding in return for being the primary sponsor. As a result, the Ridgeway Cleaning logo appeared on every bit of promotional material for the Christmas fair. But Alice hadn't had a conversation with Mariella yet. She always seemed to be in a hurry, pressed for time, and often sent her son, Ben, to budget meetings with the mayor and the Blithedale Future Fund.

"She's a busy woman," Alice remarked, nodding at the trailer.

Ona said, "She runs the cleaning company, handles staffing for this event, and I hear she's on the board of two other companies in Tilbury Town."

"She's lucky her son is so involved."

"Yeah, he's sort of her second in command."

Alice, Becca, and Ona wandered over to the floats to admire the different sculptures, and Alice watched Ben on the ladder, with Mohammad holding the bottom, as he tried to fix the elf's loose arm.

"That'll have to do," Ben said.

"If there's wind, Mr. Ridgeway, it will fall off again." Ben looked down with a raised eyebrow, and Mohammad grimaced. "Sorry. Ben."

"No problem, Mohammad. If it falls, we'll fix it again."

Loud music blasted from the area around the stage, and Alice turned toward it.

Ona grinned. "The show's about to begin. Let's go."

As the three of them headed back toward the gate, Alice saw two people in the distance crossing the path between the trailers. The woman in the light-blue Ridgeway Cleaning jacket must be Mariella Ridgeway. She was guiding a Santa impersonator up the stairs to the stage, apparently preparing him for the show.

Alice's stomach churned as she recognized him.

It was Bunce.

CHAPTER 5

"*T*his is great, isn't it?"

Ona was beaming, but Alice bit her lip and looked around nervously. A few paces away, Todd Townsend was clutching a notebook and pen with obvious anticipation. He wasn't the only person ready for the show to begin. Most everyone else in the crowd was gazing up at the stage.

Speakers blared upbeat Christmas tunes.

Becca nudged her. "What's eating you, Alice? You look distracted."

"I'm worried, that's all. There's so much riding on this..."

And Bunce—rotten luck personified—is waiting in the wings.

"Everyone's happy." Becca gestured at the surrounding crowd. "The vendors can hardly keep up with sales. The Ridgeway Cleaning crew are doing an amazing job as event staff. We've got more Santas than most Santa conventions..."

"And more journalists, too," Todd added with a grimace, edging over to them. "It's not just *The Tilbury Times* that's sent its people. We've got reporters from half-a-dozen news sites—local, regional, even national."

Alice's stomach tightened into a knot. This should've

made her thrilled—it was more promotion than Blithedale had ever had, and exactly what they'd hoped for—but what if Bunce brought disaster with him and it turned into national news?

"Half-a-dozen news sources reporting the same dull news," Todd said. He shook his head. "Now, what we really need is a big, juicy story that'll set Blithedale's Christmas fair apart."

"Like what?" Becca said with a raised eyebrow.

A smile spread across Todd's face. "Like that."

The crowd began to cheer and applaud. On stage, a man in a Santa costume stumbled onto the stage, tripping over a wire. It was Bunce. He straightened up and headed for the microphone at center stage. He grabbed it and it whined, making Alice wince.

"Ho, ho, ho," he said, and the microphone crackled. He sounded as jolly as Scrooge. He might as well have said, "Bah humbug."

Still, people cheered and clapped. He waved at the audience, which seemed more like a dismissive gesture than a greeting. Then he said, "As Blithedale's official Santa Claus, I'm *delighted* to kick off this year's *festive* Christmas fair." He delivered the words "delighted" and "festive" with his characteristic sneer. And he sounded even less pleased when he pointed toward the wings and said, "Please welcome our host, Abigail Digby."

More cheering and clapping.

As Bunce shuffled off stage, Abigail Digby entered. She wore high heels, a Scottish tartan skirt, and a black top with a red scarf. Over that, a red jacket. She looked like she got fashion tips from the British Royal Family. And she waved at the crowd as if she were the Queen.

"Oh, thank you," she said. "You're so kind. Thank you."

She turned her smiling face this way and then that, as if

she didn't want anyone to feel deprived of her grace. Finally, she held up a hand to stop the audience from cheering, though the crowd had, in fact, gone quiet a while ago.

"I'm honored to serve as your host for the annual Blithedale Christmas Fair." She beamed again at the audience. "We have brought vendors from around town—even across the state—to provide you with delicious treats and handcrafted..." Her smile faltered a little. She dipped a hand into her coat and brought out a stack of notecards. She shuffled through them. Smiled again. "...arts and crafts. And we have a wonderful, wonderful parade of horse-drawn floats. To tell us more about the event, please give a big round of applause for our main sponsor, Ridgeway Cleaning, and its CEO, Mary-Ann Ridgeway."

Mariella Ridgeway emerged from the wings and strode to the microphone as Abigail Digby inched backward to relinquish a little space. But not much.

"Hello, everyone," Mariella said, all business. Then glanced at Abigail before turning back to the audience. "I'm *Mariella* Ridgeway. People say I run Ridgeway Cleaning. In reality, it's the cleaners who run this business, the men and women who work hard every day to make municipal buildings and businesses clean and safe. They are the true Santa's helpers, making homes and workplaces clean and cozy. Please give them all a round of applause."

The audience clapped and cheered.

Mariella said, "You'll see my colleagues all around you. We all wear blue jackets. And we're here to make sure you have a wonderful time."

The crowd cheered. Mariella flashed a brief smile. Then went on. "We've created the floats for the parade. Each one is made of repurposed waste materials, and when the Christmas fair ends, every sculpture will be recycled."

More cheers and applause.

"We're also sponsoring this year's Santa Claus Contest. Throughout the fair, you'll see men and women dressed as Santa Claus. We've equipped each with a bag of presents, small treats for your kids—all courtesy of Ridgeway Cleaning. The Santas are here to make your experience—and your kids' experience—as festive as possible."

Alice sighed. *Except for one Santa...*

"At the end of the fair," Mariella continued, "you will all have a chance to vote for this year's number one Santa—the one person who most embodies the spirit of Christmas."

Even more cheers and applause from the audience. Someone called out, "Ho, ho, ho," and people laughed.

"Thank you," Mariella said, saluting the audience. "And have a merry Christmas!"

As soon as Mariella walked away from the microphone, Abigail stepped into her place. She emitted a little laugh, a clear bell-like tinkle that sounded pretty but conveyed little emotion. "How delightful. And speaking of the Santa contest, here's Mr. Vickers to tell us more about it."

A man stepped onto the stage. He was lean and pale—almost as pasty as Bunce—and sported a close-cropped beard with flecks of white. His eyes had dark rings under them.

He grabbed the microphone and said gruffly, "Here's how it works..."

But before Alice could hear what he was going to say, someone tugged at her sleeve and whispered, "Alice, please, gome guick."

Chief Jimbo stood next to her. His bloodshot eyes were wide and darted this way and that, as if he were terrified someone would hear what he was saying.

"What's going on?"

"Gome," he repeated. "Gome now."

Alice exchanged a glance with Ona and then Becca, who

both nodded at her. The three of them followed Chief Jimbo through the crowd. He took them across the spectator area to the gate by the stage.

Inside the staff-only area, he hurried toward the trailer marked "Santa Claus Contestants." Down by the floats, someone was standing on a ladder. Outside the trailer stood a group of Santas. They huddled together, speaking in animated voices and gesturing toward the trailer.

As Chief Jimbo approached and they saw his uniform, they stepped aside, and he climbed the short stairs to the door. He pulled at the handle, but it seemed to be stuck. He pulled and then it gave way. As he yanked the door open, he stumbled off the steps. Alice caught him and put a steadying hand on his back.

"Thanks," he muttered.

Alice noticed his hands. They were trembling.

He pointed inside the trailer.

Alice stepped past him.

The trailer had a table at one end with coffee urns and a tray full of cookies and donuts. At the other end stood a dressing screen and a clothing rack—a place for Santas to change in and out of their costumes. Nothing unusual. But when Alice stepped further into the trailer, she saw the man in a Santa costume sitting at the table behind the coffee urns.

The man called Wade.

He sagged in his chair, his head cocked at an odd angle, as if he'd passed out. But the froth at his mouth suggested otherwise. And the pallor of his face told her at once what had happened.

Chief Jimbo confirmed it.

"He's dead," he said. "Mr. Ridgeway is dead."

Alice did a double take.

"Ridgeway? As in Ridgeway Cleaning?"

"Wade Ridgeway," Chief Jimbo said. "Mariella's husband. Ben's dad." He groaned. "This couldn't get worse…"

Alice was inclined to agree.

But then a voice outside the trailer froze her guts, making her reassess how bad things could get.

"You can't keep the press from the truth," Todd was saying as he forced his way past Becca and Ona and stepped into the trailer.

His eyes widened. Then he smiled. "Yes! Finally, a juicy story."

CHAPTER 6

*L*enny Stout, the county coroner, wasn't wearing his usual rumpled, gray suit. He was wearing a festive knit sweater with a pattern of Christmas trees and Winnie-the-Pooh characters. He had been enjoying a day off at the fair when Alice called and he'd rushed to the staff-only area.

"He's dead," Lenny confirmed. "Not that you need me to tell you that."

With a little coaxing from Alice, Becca, and Ona, Chief Jimbo secured the scene of the crime, forcing Todd to step out of the trailer. By then, a crowd was gathering. Lots of people in light-blue jackets, others in Santa Claus costumes.

In the distance, Alice noticed that it was Ben Ridgeway on the ladder by the floats. He stopped working and turned, apparently curious about the hubbub by the trailer. He clambered down the ladder.

"What's going on?" he said, as he came jogging toward her. "Is everything OK?"

Chief Jimbo opened his mouth to speak, but no words came.

Alice said, "Ben, could we talk? Maybe in the management trailer across the way?"

Ben nodded.

"I'll geep an eye on things here," Chief Jimbo muttered and blew his nose into his handkerchief.

In contrast to the space for the Santa impersonators, the Management & Logistics trailer looked like a mobile office. There were three desks with desktop computers and printers. Cork boards on the walls. A white board. A table for meetings.

Mohammad was standing at the white board checking off a long to-do list. Mariella sat at a computer, typing away.

"Mrs. Ridgeway," Alice said, and she said, "Call me Mariella," without looking up from her screen. Alice took a deep breath. This was absurd. She was a bookseller, not a cop. She shouldn't be informing next of kin. But if she didn't pick up Chief Jimbo's slack, no one would, and Ben and his mom deserved to know what had happened.

"It's about your husband."

Mariella let out a short, exasperated sigh and turned in her chair. "Now what?"

Alice looked at Ben, whose face was one big question mark. Then she looked back at Mariella and said, "They found Wade in the trailer across the way. He's dead."

There was a clatter as Mohammad dropped his pen.

Ben drew in a sharp breath of air. "Dad? Dead? You're sure?"

Then he swiveled around and bolted out of the trailer, his scarf trailing behind him.

Mohammad, looking horrified, hesitated a moment. Then followed Ben.

Outside, Alice could hear Ben's voice, raised. "Let me in— I want to see my dad. Let me in."

But Mariella hadn't moved. She sat still, her hands resting in her lap, her gaze fixed on something in the distance.

"Mariella?"

Her eyes focused on Alice.

"This—" She sighed. "—complicates matters. So tell me, how can I be helpful?"

All business.

"Your husband is dead," Alice said. "You understand that, don't you?"

"I understand. I'm not in shock. I'm not even that surprised. But I recognize that this poses a risk to the Christmas fair, since it may upset people. As the event's main sponsor, I'm available to help mitigate any fallout from this —" She paused. "—tragedy."

She sounded like a politician or a press release, not a grieving widow. But Alice reminded herself that people reacted in a million different ways to the loss of a loved one. Sometimes grief arrived later.

"You said you weren't surprised…"

"Let's not speak ill of the dead. If there's something practical I can help with, let me know. For instance, I can identify the body. Isn't that a thing you'll need me to do?"

Alice nodded. "I'll check with the county coroner."

"Great, thanks. Let me know."

Mariella turned back to her computer and continued to type.

Alice retreated from the trailer, dazed, feeling oddly like a subordinate who'd been dismissed by her boss.

Back at the Santa Claus trailer, Ona and Becca stood guard by the entrance to keep the curious out. But also to keep Ben Ridgeway at bay.

"I want to see him," he said.

Lenny appeared in the doorway. "And you will. But this is

a crime scene. No unauthorized personnel enters. Except... you."

He'd spotted Alice and now gestured for her to approach. She followed him into the trailer, and he mumbled, "This is a mess, and as usual, Chief Jimbo isn't doing much to help."

Chief Jimbo stood against a wall, hands in his pockets, sniffling.

He looks more grief-stricken than the widow...

"Look at this," Lenny said, grabbing Alice by the arm and leading her to the table with the dead man.

It was nuts that the county coroner was including her in the investigation. But given how little Chief Jimbo had done to solve past murder cases—and how much Alice had contributed to catching the killers—she understood that Lenny now saw her in a different light.

She didn't have time to reflect too much on the absurdity of the situation, however, because Lenny was pointing out crime scene details.

"Poisoned. I'm guessing he ingested it." Lenny pointed to a cup of hot chocolate. "I'll run tests on the cup and the thermos next to it. I'll also check the coffee urns and other beverages, though my money is on the hot cocoa. The sweetness masks poison pretty well."

Alice studied the table full of beverages and snacks.

"Anyone could stop and have a drink and snack. Was Wade a random victim, or was he targeted?"

"Good question. We won't know for sure until we get the toxicology report. But Santa impersonators have been drinking coffee and cocoa from this station all day, and no one's gotten sick. If a lunatic wanted to poison all the Santas, wouldn't we have a dozen dead on our hands?"

"Makes sense. But if Wade was targeted, the killer needed to make sure he drank the poison. How?" She thought for a moment. "The killer could've served the poisoned cocoa."

"We'll check for fingerprints, of course," Lenny said, and turned toward Chief Jimbo. "Won't we?"

Chief Jimbo nodded.

Alice looked around the room. Near one of the table legs sat a sack. The sack bore a discreetly placed corporate logo that said, "Ridgeway Cleaning." Throughout the fair, she'd seen Santas carrying sacks with presents. These were the bags of gifts that each Santa was equipped with, courtesy of Ridgeway Cleaning. But Wade hadn't been carrying the sack when she saw him earlier—running down Main Street, threatening the man called Lewis.

"We should check the bag of presents, too," she said.

"That one's full of voting slips for the Santa contest," Lenny said, pointing to the bag. "Belongs to Vickers. It doesn't look like Wade had a Santa bag."

"And there's something missing." Alice racked her brain. Then realized what it was. She looked around the room, behind the table, then behind the dressing screen. "The leather pouch he was carrying. It's gone."

CHAPTER 7

*O*utside the windows of the What the Dickens Diner, darkness had fallen. Blithedale was a ghostly landscape under dim streetlights, occasionally flashing to life as the headlights of cars swept past. Snowflakes speckled the light.

As they finished their dinner—Becca's meatloaf special with mashed potatoes and cranberry sauce—Alice filled Becca and Ona in on what she'd experienced: first spotting Wade rushing down Main Street and later threatening a man named Lewis.

"…so, you see, the missing leather pouch might be important," Alice said.

They were sitting in a booth. Ona, next to Alice on the red leatherette seat, had kicked off her shoes and pulled up her legs under her. Becca faced them from across the table.

"What could be in the pouch?" Becca asked.

Alice shrugged. "Documents."

"But what kinds of documents?"

"I don't know. We don't even know why someone wanted to kill Wade Ridgeway, unless it was about money. First thing I've got to do is find that guy, Lewis, and see how he's connected to Wade."

She stopped herself.

"I mean, the police will need to find him."

"Oh, come on," Ona said. "Can we please skip the whole part where you refuse to investigate? Chief Jimbo's not going to solve this murder."

"There's always the county sheriff or state police. Besides, this is serious. If we bungle this murder investigation, the authorities might shut down the Christmas fair. Or people might panic, and then what will we do?"

Susan, the waitress, cleared the table, and Becca promised to relieve her in a minute.

"You're right," Becca said, turning back to Alice. "We've invested a lot in this fair. But that's the reason I think you should get involved."

"The cops are professionals."

"We have one cop in this town," Ona said. "And I dare you to call him 'professional' to my face."

"My point is," Alice said with a sigh, "that I'm definitely not a professional. I'm a bookseller. We need someone to handle this with kid gloves. We need the state police. We need—"

The door to the diner flew open, sending snow flurries cartwheeling across the linoleum floor. Mayor MacDonald stepped inside. He wore a long white winter coat and carried a cane, looking, as usual, like a Mark Twain impersonator. Lenny Stout, the county coroner, followed close behind. The two of them continued an argument that must've begun outside.

"State police," the mayor made a sweeping gesture, as if to clear away the idea. "Don't even mention the state police."

"But Chief Jimbo isn't—"

"Jimbo is our chief of police. He'll do fine."

"We need better than *fine*."

The two men approached their booth. Becca got out of her seat and offered it to them, excusing herself—she had to get back to work.

Mayor MacDonald slid into the booth, followed by Lenny.

"I've covered for Chief Jimbo in the past," Lenny said. "But there's too much attention on this fair. Did you see how much press turned up?"

Mayor MacDonald winced. "Under normal circumstances, that would be a cause for celebration…"

Lenny said, "But these aren't normal circumstances. Which is why we need help. If you don't like the state police, then let's call the county sheriff and his deputies."

"The last time we did that, Sheriff Carl Cutter shut down half of Blithedale."

"Sheriff Calcutta?" Alice asked.

"Sheriff Carl," Mayor MacDonald clarified, "Cutter. He's the county sheriff, based out of Tilbury Town. And he's so subtle he'd use a sledgehammer to kill an ant."

"Sheriff Cutter does a decent job," Lenny said, but his eyes drifted away and his shoulders slumped. "Mostly, anyway."

Mayor MacDonald clearly saw his chance. He leaned forward and slapped the tabletop. "Chief Jimbo will lead the investigation. But I agree, Lenny. He needs help."

"Good," Lenny said. "Glad we agree."

"And he'll get help. He can deputize Alice and she can help."

"Me?" Alice said.

"Jimbo can't deputize Alice," Lenny protested. "You know that, Mayor. He's not a sheriff. A chief of police doesn't deputize citizens."

Mayor MacDonald made a dismissive gesture. "You know what I mean. Anyway, it's ideal. Uniforms and regulations won't constrain Alice. She'll be free to ask around without raising suspicion and sending the killer into hiding. Am I right?"

"Well..." Lenny said, rubbing the back of his neck. "You're not wrong."

"Hey, do I have a say in all this?" Alice asked.

The two men looked at her as if they'd seen her for the first time.

"Of course you do," Mayor MacDonald said. "If you have a better solution, I'm all ears."

He leaned back and crossed his arms, staring at Alice with a formidable frown. It reminded her of courtroom dramas where the prosecution made its closing argument, resting its case. Becca had returned to the booth and stood over them, gazing down at Alice in anticipation. Next to her, Ona was watching her, too. The whole jury was waiting for her to say something.

"What about Chief Jimbo?" she said. "He must have an opinion about all this."

Mayor MacDonald smiled, his eyes glittering with triumph.

"Oh, sure. Great idea. Let's consult Chief Jimbo."

CHAPTER 8

*A*s Mayor MacDonald's SUV pulled up to the curb by Chief Jimbo's home, Alice peered out the back window. She knew this neighborhood. It was where Susan, the waitress at the diner, lived. Rows of modest ranch-style homes featured small, snow-covered front yards and single-car garages. Chief Jimbo's cruiser stood parked in the driveway.

Mayor MacDonald, looking in the rearview mirror at his two passengers in the back, cited the asking price for several houses in the area.

"Affordable homes."

"For some," Alice said, thinking of her own modest savings.

She'd spent most of her savings on setting up and stocking the bookstore, and although a generous rent at Ona's inn meant she could put money aside, she didn't have enough for a down payment on a home. Especially not since she'd sunk additional money into the fund for the Christmas fair, expecting to make it back in increased sales.

"I can't get involved in this," Alice whispered to Ona, not for the first time.

"You'll do fine. Better than our chief of police, anyway. You've investigated murders before."

"But it's not just about the murder…"

Having put the car in park, Mayor MacDonald turned in his seat to look back at her. "You're right, Alice. It's not just about the murder. It's about how we pull together as a town. You know, someone once said, 'It takes a village—'"

"Oh, please," Ona said.

"Yeah, that's enough, Mayor," Alice said. "Let's go talk to Jimbo."

Mayor MacDonald opened his door as Alice and Ona got out of the backseat. As they trudged up the driveway, Alice glanced back, squinting against the wet pinpricks of snow on her face. Letters on the side of the mayor's SUV advertised his company, "MacDonald Realty." Blithedale's only realtor was also its mayor. There was a conflict of interest there, but no one in town seemed to question it. To Alice herself, it was secondary to how the mayor hired the young chief of police based on family credentials. The old chief of police had been James Sapling, Sr., and James Sapling, Jr.—or Jimbo, as he preferred to be called—proved that not all talents pass from generation to generation.

Mayor MacDonald knocked on the front door with the head of his cane.

"There is a doorbell, you know," Ona said, an amused twinkle in her eye. It matched the sparkle of her rhinestone-decorated eyepatch. "But then why carry around a fancy cane, right?"

Mayor MacDonald frowned, but otherwise ignored her. They weren't on the best of terms, the mayor and Ona, and a moment like this reminded Alice of it. As well as running the Pemberley Inn, Ona built tiny houses, like the one she'd made for Alice's bookshop. But although he'd made an exception with Wonderland Books, the mayor refused to change the municipal building code to allow for more tiny houses downtown, effectively stalling Ona's side hustle.

A voice, muffled by distance as well as by the front door, responded to the knock: "Gome in. Door's open."

Mayor MacDonald pushed open the front door and the three of them stepped inside, stomping their boots on the welcome mat to remove the snow.

A corridor led to a kitchen. Sounds came from the living room, off to the left. On a flatscreen TV, *The Rockford Files* was on and Chief Jimbo lay on a big couch across from the TV, covered in a blanket that was littered with balled-up tissues. His nose was red, his eyes rheumy. He gave his visitors a puzzled, puppy-eyed look.

Alice said, "We're here to talk about the murder of Wade Ridgeway."

Chief Jimbo seemed to sink deeper into the couch. "I don't feel so good...this virus...I think I may need to go to the hospital." He sniffled. His voice was nasal, though Alice wondered whether he might be exaggerating it. He said, "You should gall Sheriff Gutter. Get his help."

Alice nodded, seeing a chance to step back from this mess. "I agree. Sheriff Cutter sounds like a professional—"

"Excellent news, Jimbo," Mayor MacDonald said, cutting her off. "Alice here has volunteered to help with the investigation."

Chief Jimbo's eyes widened. He pushed himself up. "Yes," he said with surprising energy for someone apparently suffering from a deadly virus. "Alice is perfect for the job. She gan lead the investigation. She gan do it."

Alice waved her hands in protest. "I'm not leading anything. You're the chief of police."

"Of course," Mayor MacDonald said. "But you'll be Jimbo's eyes and ears on the ground."

"My eyes and ears," Chief Jimbo agreed, nodding.

Alice sighed. "Can I at least think about it? Sleep on it?"

"Sure," Mayor MacDonald said. "Sleep on it. But keep in mind, the murderer won't be sleeping."

"That's not literally true," Ona said. "Killers need rest, too."

Mayor MacDonald shot her an irritated look.

Alice grabbed Ona's arm before she said something that might enrage the mayor, and they headed into the hallway. Mayor MacDonald lingered to talk to Chief Jimbo.

By the front door, Alice stopped to study a wall of framed photos, including a large photo collage. There were snapshots of Jimbo and his dad in fishing gear, holding up a big fish they'd caught. Several images depicted Jimbo at work—one where, dressed in his uniform, he was drinking coffee at the diner, and another where he was flanking Darrell Townsend, Todd's incarcerated brother who'd once run Townsend Development, as he cut the ribbon on a new building. But it was the one of Jimbo at the Christmas fair that caught her attention.

"Was this last year's fair?" she asked Ona.

Ona leaned closer to study the photograph. "That's right. Because look who's in the background."

Alice leaned close, too. The people behind Jimbo were almost all out of focus, except for two men, who were easily identifiable. One was wearing a red coat and hat—a Santa costume. It was Bunce. He was talking to a man she'd seen before.

"That's Vickers," Ona said. "You remember, right? Abigail Digby introduced him on stage today."

"Bunce and Vickers…" Alice said. Then, looking closer, added, "That's strange…"

"Nothing strange about that. Vickers organizes the Santa contest. Bunce, as you know, participated last year."

"No, it's not strange that they would be talking. But look closer."

Ona stared at the photo and then shook her head. "What?"

"Bunce is smiling. When does Bunce *ever* smile?"

Now Ona was smiling.

"What?" Alice asked. "What's so funny?"

"Think about it? Sleep on it? Can't help yourself, can you?"

Alice stared at her friend. Ona was right. Tomorrow morning, would she feel any different about the situation? She let out a sigh. "All right. Let's go find Bunce and ask him some questions."

"Yes!" Ona threw an arm around Alice's shoulders and squeezed. "Let's go catch us a killer."

CHAPTER 9

*A*lice had no idea where Bunce was staying, and no one else seemed to know. But she was in luck. The next morning, she stepped into the What the Dickens Diner to meet Ona, and as they were looking for a seat, she spotted Bunce eating breakfast.

"Let's go say hello," Alice said.

Ona grinned. "This should be fun."

Bunce was seated alone in a booth with a plate full of pancakes, scrambled eggs, bacon, hash browns, and sausage. All of it drowned in a swamp of ketchup and maple syrup. As she approached him from behind, he took a gulp of coffee, and nearly choked on it when she said his name.

He wiped his mouth with the back of his hand.

"Don't sneak up on me like that. You could give me a heart attack."

"Your breakfast is what'll give you a heart attack."

"Do you sell books or dieting advice?"

"Actually, I'm interested in what you know about Wade Ridgeway."

Alice sat down across from him, sliding into the booth to

make room for Ona. Bunce cut a slab of pancake with his fork and shoved it into his mouth. He chewed.

"So," Ona said. "Wade Ridgeway. What do you know?"

"He's dead."

"And before he died?"

"He was alive." Bunce threw down his fork. "Can't a man eat his breakfast in peace?"

On the wall by the booth hung a framed illustration from a Charles Dickens novel. Becca had decorated it with tinsel to add a bit of Christmas flair. In the illustration, a skinny little Oliver Twist held his empty bowl. The master of the parish workhouse stared goggle-eyed at the boy. The caption read, "Oliver asking for more." It struck Alice how much the workhouse master looked like Bunce.

Becca came to the booth and poured coffee for Alice and Ona.

"What a pleasure to see you, Bunce," she said innocently. A little too innocently. "I'm surprised to see you back in Blithedale."

While Bunce grumbled something inaudible, she winked at Alice and moved on to the other tables.

"Yeah, Bunce," Alice said. "You were so glad to leave Blithedale behind. Why come back now?"

"A man has his reasons."

"And they are…?"

"All right, all right. You want to know about Wade? I knew him, of course. He was a fellow Santa contestant. He was also a pain. Always hanging around and sticking his nose in other people's business, gossiping, asking questions." He narrowed his eyes at Alice. "Like someone else I know."

"Any idea why someone wanted to kill Wade?"

"As I said, he was a pain."

Ona sighed. "You're a pain and no one's killed you. What set Wade apart?"

"How should I know? I'm here for the Santa contest, that's all. Once this is over, I'll be glad to go back to my retirement in Florida."

"Speaking of the Santa contest," Alice said, "what about Vickers?"

Bunce shrugged. He picked up his fork and speared a lump of scrambled egg. As he ate, he focused on his plate. "We know each other professionally. Vickers runs the Santa contest. I'm one of the Santas. What more is there to say?"

He shoveled sausage into his mouth. Then turned his attention to demolishing the bacon.

Alice and Ona exchanged looks. Bunce wasn't telling them the truth—or he was withholding something.

Alice leaned forward. "What aren't you telling us?"

Bunce grimaced. "Nothing."

"People don't cut their bacon into tiny pieces like that. They pick it up and they eat it."

"And then they go on cholesterol meds," Ona added.

"Fine," Bunce said. "You looking for someone suspicious? Take a look at Lewis Tuttle."

"Lewis Tuttle?" Alice said.

"Yeah, he's in the Santa contest, too. And he was hanging around the Santa trailer before Wade died."

Alice realized this must be the "Lewis" that Wade threatened.

Ona said, "You're in the Santa contest, too. So are dozens of other people. And everyone was hanging around that trailer. Nothing suspicious about that."

"Wade was poisoned, right?" Bunce said. "That's what *The Blithedale Record* says."

"So what?" Alice asked.

"Well, Lewis used to run a pharmacy," Bunce said. "If anyone knows poisons, it would be Lewis."

CHAPTER 10

$\mathcal{L}$orraine Maxwell, Blithedale's head librarian, tottered into Wonderland Books, nearly collapsing under the weight of a massive box.

"Where do I put this?"

"Anywhere."

Alice moved around the counter to help. She grabbed the other side of the box and together they eased it to the floor.

"Phew," Lorraine said, straightening up.

"What's in here—bricks?"

"Books." Lorraine opened the cardboard flaps. "I packed them as tight as I could."

Alice leaned over to look inside. Lorraine wasn't kidding. She'd played a game of Tetris with the books, fitting them together so neatly that there weren't any gaps.

"More donations," Lorraine said. "Old library books taken out of circulation."

"Thank you."

"Should you be thanking me?"

With a raised eyebrow, Lorraine looked around the bookstore. Stacks of books covered the counter, and behind it, Alice had almost no room to move around—the space was crammed with boxes and books.

"It's a good problem to have," Alice said, though she bit her lip as she thought of where to put all the books.

When she first opened Wonderland Books, she'd relied on donations to supplement her new stock. She saw it as a way to get started. But the idea caught on. Locals enjoyed being generous—and clearing out their basements and attics —so they continued to deliver boxes of books. Even leaving them on the doorstep. So Ona had installed a box outside the bookstore that allowed people to make donations outside of business hours. When it rained or snowed, it kept the books dry. Usually, the box filled up during the week. But as the days crept closer to Christmas, people wanted to clear out their closets, and that included old books. The donation box was full every other morning.

"As long as you sell the books, it is a good problem," Lorraine said. "Speaking of which, I'm looking for a book."

She dug into her winter coat and pulled out a paperback.

'Tis by Frank McCourt.

"This is the sequel," she said. "I started reading it, and it's so good that I stopped."

"You stopped because it's good?"

"So I can read the first one first."

Luckily, Alice stocked the first book, *Angela's Ashes*. She found it under M on the shelves. She usually carried a copy of *Angela's Ashes*—it was a classic memoir—though she rarely stocked the sequel, so Lorraine had been lucky to get her hands on the second book first.

"Here, you can have this for free." As she handed Lorraine the book, she gestured at the giant box. "It's the least I can do to pay you back for your generosity."

"Don't be silly," Lorraine said in her sternest librarian voice. "If you give away books for free, you can't survive. I'll pay you."

As she counted the bills, she said, "We don't have a copy at the library. I could've done an interlibrary loan, but I'm eager to start right away." Then she leaned close, as if wanting to share a secret. "The strange thing is that I got this book as a present."

"Why's that strange?"

"It was anonymous. Someone left it in my mailbox. No note or anything. But it was nicely wrapped with a ribbon and everything."

Alice smiled. "What a nice surprise. Don't you think it was Sandy?"

It seemed most likely that Sandy Spiegel, Lorraine's best friend, would do something that nice for her.

But Lorraine shook her head.

"Sandy's lousy at secrets. And this isn't the sort of book she'd get me."

She pocketed her newly bought copy of *Angela's Ashes* and turned to leave. But Alice reached out and touched her arm, stopping her.

"Do you know Lewis Tuttle?"

"Not well, no. But I heard about his difficulties, of course."

"What difficulties?"

"He used to own a pharmacy on the road to Tilbury Town, but it went out of business."

"Any idea where I could find him?"

Lorraine shook her head. "He used to live by his pharmacy, but his house went into foreclosure."

After Lorraine left, Alice put music on the wall-mounted speakers, and soon a cozy soundtrack of Christmas songs played softly as she flipped through book after book. She added price tags and shelved a dozen books before running out of space. After that, she stacked the ones she'd priced behind the counter. The rejects—including half a dozen copies of *Digital Fortress* by Dan Brown—went back into boxes.

But only half her mind was on the books. Periodically, she received a text message from Ona or Becca about the investigation. She'd told them what Lorraine had said about Lewis. Becca confirmed it—she'd heard the same story. But neither she nor Ona knew where Lewis was now.

Alice sent a message filling them in on what Lorraine had told her. It wasn't much to go by. And they still didn't know where Lewis Tuttle was.

As Alice continued to sort through the books, customers came and went. Out-of-towners, mostly. Then Althea Strong stepped into the store.

Althea was the lead singer and banjo player in the Pointed Firs, Blithedale's popular bluegrass band.

Althea held out a paperback. "Hey, Alice, see this?"

It was a book by Madeleine L'Engle called *A Severed Wasp*.

"I know L'Engle's classic, *A Wrinkle in Time*," Alice said, taking the book from Althea and examining it. "But I don't know this one."

"It's great. I started it last night. It's about this pianist in her seventies. Not the kind of book I usually pick up, but I couldn't put it down. I finished it last night. Now I want to read the first book, *The Small Rain*. This is the sequel."

"I noticed a used copy of a Madeleine L'Engle somewhere here. But I doubt it's the book you're looking for..."

Alice turned around and crouched down, examining the spines of the stacked books. Then spotted L'Engle's name.

"Well, what are the chances?" She straightened up and

turned back to Althea, showing her the cover of Madeleine L'Engle's *The Small Rain*. "This is the one, isn't it?"

Althea beamed. "Yes!" As she got out cash to pay for it, she said, "Seriously, what *are* the chances? First, I get *A Severed Wasp* as a present—some Good Samaritan left it in my mailbox, beautifully wrapped, but no note—and now you actually have the first book. I should check my horoscope. Maybe I can expect good things this Christmas."

Alice frowned. *Funny coincidence.*

But she pushed the thought aside. Althea was about to leave, and Alice needed to know if she'd seen Lewis Tuttle.

"The pharmacy guy? No, no idea where he is. Such a shame about his business going bust. He had a section with Scandinavian products, and there was this face cream I loved. He imported it from Denmark or Sweden, and I can't find it online…" Althea shook her head. "Listen to me, selfishly complaining about my face cream when the real tragedy is that Lewis lost the business he loved."

After she left, Alice leaned against the counter, staring into the middle distance. Now she considered Althea's book again. *How strange,* she thought. *Could it be the same Good Samaritan that gave Lorraine a book? Anything else would be too much of a coincidence.*

She shook her head. *You're seeing mysteries everywhere. It's probably just a coincidence. After all, it's Christmas—lots of people play secret Santa, don't they?*

But half an hour later, Andrea Connor from Bonsai & Pie came charging through the door.

"Alice, I need your help."

Breathless, because she needed to get back to her Christmas fair stall as quickly as possible, she explained that someone had left her an anonymous gift. A well-wrapped present was waiting for her in the stall when she opened it this morning. And inside was a book.

"So I started reading it," she said, "and now I'm totally hooked. But the thing is—"

"It's the sequel?" Alice said.

"Huh. How did you know that?"

"Lucky guess."

Andrea showed her the book. It was a fantasy novel called *First Rider's Call* by Kristen Britain. Alice didn't know the author. She was also sure she didn't stock any books by Kristen Britain.

"I can look among the donations," she told Andrea, "but it's not likely I have it. I can order it for you, though."

Andrea's face fell. "Aw, I was hoping to have something to read while I sit my stall."

"Let me check."

It took two minutes of looking through the books behind the counter. There it was, in a box she hadn't sorted through yet: Kristen Britain's *Green Rider*, the first in her fantasy series.

After Andrea paid for the book and hurried off, Alice stared at the stacks of books. This was no coincidence. The Frank McCourt incident didn't feel far-fetched, but the L'Engle and Britain books turning up among the donations seemed too convenient. Something strange was happening.

Who's this Good Samaritan?

She'd mixed up the books from the donation box and the ones that people had brought in. She had no way of knowing who had left her the L'Engle and Britain books.

Another mystery. She sighed. *Why are there so many mysteries in Blithedale?*

A mystery book in one of her boxes caught her eye— Joanne Fluke's *Raspberry Danish Murder*—and a vague idea niggled at the back of her mind.

Danish. Scandinavian face cream. Lewis Tuttle...

She was sure she knew someone with a Danish connection.

A jolt went through her as she remembered, and she grabbed her phone and fired off a message to Ona.

> Woodlander Bar tonight? I've got a hunch.

> I love your hunches. And I love the Woodlander. It's a date!

CHAPTER 11

*D*eep in the Blithedale Woods, two tiny houses, both built by Ona, faced each other. One was Under the Greenwood Tree, a new restaurant run by the young, talented chef, Dylan. The other, the Woodlander Bar, had been there for longer.

After dinner at the diner, Alice and Ona had driven into the woods. Becca, who had to work, as usual, couldn't joint them.

As Alice got out of Ona's pickup truck, her boots crunching into snow, she said, "If anyone knows Lewis Tuttle, I bet it's Thor."

A roof kept much of the snow off the area between the two tiny houses. Patio heaters glowed, fighting a futile battle against the cold air. And yet a few hardy people sat huddled under blankets at tables, warmed by the glow of the heaters, while their hands wrapped around mugs of hot mulled wine. It was too frigid to eat a meal outside, but it looked cozy under those blankets.

Alice was striding through the snow toward the Woodlander Bar when one of the huddled figures wrapped in blankets called her name. A thick woolen hat, a heavy scarf, and that mound of blankets almost made him unrecognizable.

"Oh, Mayor MacDonald," she said, stopping. "I didn't recognize you."

"I feel like a mummy."

"But you look warm."

"What I am," he said, looking left and right, "is hiding."

He beckoned for her to come closer, and she crouched down by his side. Ona stood a few paces away, hands on her hips and an amused look on her face.

"Hiding?" Alice said. "Hiding from who?"

"The press. They're hounding me for answers about Wade's death."

"Todd's giving you a hard time."

"Todd? No, no. It's *The Tilbury Times* folks and the other journalists who are pressing me for answers. Todd is fine. We've made a deal. He ran a cursory report on Wade's death, but will delay any follow-ups in return for an exclusive interview once you catch the killer."

It was typical of the mayor that he'd make a deal with Todd to manage the media sensation around a murder. But something about how he'd looked at her when he said "exclusive interview" made her wonder. And when he said "you," he meant both Alice and Chief Jimbo, right?

"What do you mean, exclusive interview?"

The blankets rose and fell as he shrugged. "Todd will want to talk to the lead investigator."

"Which is Chief Jimbo."

Mayor MacDonald raised an eyebrow. "Do you think Todd or anyone else is going to believe that? No, my dear. You're the primary on this. And you've got to get a move on. You can't be dilly-dallying and hanging around bars with Ona—not if you're going to catch a killer."

He gave Ona a disapproving look.

With a sigh, Alice straightened up. "Don't worry. We're working on it."

As she and Ona headed toward the entrance to the Woodlander Bar, Alice said, "How did I go from average citizen to lead investigator?"

Ona laughed. "Don't you love Blithedale?"

A man darted out of the bar, narrowly avoiding a collision with Alice. He mumbled an apology and hurried off. She turned, staring after him.

There was no mistaking him. It was Lewis Tuttle.

"Hey, wait," she called out.

"I'll be right with you," he responded. "Just clearing the tables."

He picked up empty mugs and glasses from tables and arranged them on a tray.

"Huh," Alice said.

"Thor's inside," Ona said. "Let's see what he says about Lewis."

Inside the tiny house, customers sat at small tables. Candles on ledges flickered. A cheerful bonsai Christmas tree stood on the bar counter. Overhead speakers piped bluegrass holiday tunes. Alice recognized the music. It was by Althea's band, the Pointed Firs.

Thor was at the bar, pouring a drink from a shaker into a martini glass. He smiled when he saw them.

"What can I make you?"

He was model handsome with long, blond hair, like one of those hunky guys on the cover of romance novels. His unusual name wasn't so unusual in Denmark, where his parents had come from, he'd once told her, and it was this Danish connection that made Alice think he might know Lewis.

"We were looking for Lewis, actually."

"Lewis? Well, he'll be here in a second. Why do you want

57

to see Lewis?"

Alice leaned close to him, not wanting all the customers in the tiny house bar to hear.

"I saw Lewis talking to Wade before he was killed."

Thor frowned. "That's bad."

"Why do you say that?"

"Because Lewis has had enough trouble already." He sighed. "Go easy on him, Alice. He's had a rough time in the past couple of years, but he's a hard worker and a good guy."

"Have you known him for a long time?"

"When I first moved to Blithedale, I went to his pharmacy and discovered that he has family in Sweden. He's traveled a lot in Norway, Denmark, and Sweden, and we got to talking about Scandinavia. As soon as I mentioned I was hoping to open a bar, he introduced me to local business people, which ultimately helped me launch the Woodlander. Honestly, he was a big help."

At that moment, Lewis came through the door, burdened by the tray full of mugs and glasses, and he made his way to the bar, where he handed it over to Thor.

"What can I do now?" he asked.

"Lewis, my friends Alice and Ona want to talk to you."

Lewis looked at Alice, his face open and frank. "Have I met you before? Oh. You're the owner of Wonderland Books. I read about you in *The Blithedale Record*."

Alice winced. "Please don't believe anything Todd wrote about me."

"I take his journalism with a grain of salt," Lewis said. "Besides, the Blithedale grapevine tells me Wonderland is a wonderful bookstore. I can't wait to drop by and buy some books when..." He trailed off. Then added, "Anyway, why did you want to talk to me?"

A customer came to the bar to order another drink.

Alice said, "Lewis, can we find a private place to talk?"

Lewis looked at Thor. Thor said, "Go ahead. Everything's under control here, Lewis. Take your time."

Outside, Alice, Ona, and Lewis found a distant table beneath a patio heater and sat down.

Alice got straight to the point. "I overheard you talking to Wade at the Christmas fair."

"You overheard...?" Lewis's eyes widened. "Me and Wade...?"

"Is there anything you'd like to tell us?"

Lewis, tight-lipped, shook his head.

Ona said, "Chief Jimbo has deputized Alice to help with the investigation into Wade's death."

"Can he do that?" Lewis asked.

"He can't really," Alice said. "But he has. I'm hoping you'll talk to us even if we have no authority to make you talk."

Lewis looked at her, then at Ona, apparently trying to make up his mind. His hands moved restlessly in his lap. Then something in him settled, and he sighed.

"All right, I knew Wade."

"You were friends?"

Lewis snorted. "Wade didn't have friends."

"When I overheard you, you were talking about money."

"That's right. Money. Wade didn't care about friends. He cared about money."

Alice kept quiet. Ona stirred next to her, but she raised a hand, gently warning her to remain silent. She sensed Lewis had more to say.

And he did.

"I used to own a pharmacy on the road to Tilbury Town." He gazed off into the middle distance. "A sweet little place, all my own. My customers were happy. They told me so. 'How nice to see you, Mr. Tuttle. Thank you, Mr. Tuttle. What would I do without your little pharmacy, Mr. Tuttle?'" He heaved a heavy sigh. "But the customers didn't all come back.

More and more people ordered things online. The big pharmacies in Tilbury Town did the rest. I dove headfirst from black into red. I was sure it was a temporary setback. I was desperate. That was when I met Wade."

"He loaned you money."

Lewis nodded. "He came in one day, browsing the pharmacy, chatting. Told me what a great place I had. But how tough the economy was, and that led me to confess to him about the problems I was having. 'Hey, it would be a genuine tragedy if this place shut down,' he tells me. 'I guess you could weather the storm if you had some extra cash.' He seemed so friendly, so generous."

"But there was a catch?"

"Isn't there always?" Lewis made a face. "He told me the loan would be interest free—'at least for a while.' Those were his words. I was a fool. I believed I could turn my business around. Instead, things got worse. Fewer and fewer customers. Bigger and bigger losses. Until finally I had to close my pharmacy for good."

"And then Wade wanted his money back?"

"No. He looked me up three months after my business went under and said he didn't expect me to pay the loan back at once. I was relieved at first. But then he said that he'd naturally have to charge me monthly interest on the loan."

"How much?"

"Ninety percent."

"Wait, did you say 9 percent?"

"No, 90 percent."

Ona cut in: "That's outrageous!"

Lewis nodded. "But I felt trapped. I was glad he didn't demand the money. I told myself I'd have a job within a month and I'd pay him back. But finding a job proved hard. And the minimum wage jobs I finally found—usually two at a time—cover rent and food, and not much more. I made

A CHRISTMAS TO DIE FOR

small payments to Wade, but they barely covered the accruing interest."

"Then you joined the Santa contest…"

"I thought maybe I could win and then the prize money—it's a lot of cash—could help me pay off the loan."

"But Wade demanded the money sooner. He threatened you. What was he going to do if you didn't pay him back?"

Lewis looked away. "It doesn't matter now, does it?"

Alice reached across and grabbed his arm. She didn't grip him firmly, but it still jolted him. His attention snapped back to her. He was clearly skittish.

Gently, she said, "It does matter, Lewis. Wade's dead. Someone killed him."

"That's right," Lewis said with a sigh. "He's gone, and so is my debt to him. I've dropped out of the Santa contest. Why gamble on getting a big payout when I don't have my debt to Wade anymore? I'm better off spending the time working regular jobs. So I got this temporary job at Thor's bar."

"It can't hurt to tell me what he was threatening to do. But it might help us catch the killer."

Lewis rubbed his chin, considering. Then said, "All right. Wade had photos. Compromising photos." He let out a long, deep sigh. "Years ago, I took part in SantaCon in New York City, and I got drunk, and lost control. Urinated on a Christmas tree. Passed out half-naked in an Irish pub. I used to drink too much. I don't anymore. But somehow Wade got hold of those photos. He was going to share them with *The Blithedale Record* and anyone else who'd print them. He would've ruined my chances at winning the Santa contest—and probably made my job hunt even harder."

"Why would he do that?"

Lewis shrugged. "He wanted me to keep paying him indefinitely."

"Makes sense," Ona said. "With 90 percent interest, you'd

be a long-term cash cow for him. He'd make back the money on that loan in no time." She grimaced. "That bastard."

"Lewis," Alice said. "Thank you for telling us the truth."

"Happy to." Lewis smiled, though it was a weak, faltering thing. "A friend of Thor's is a friend of mine. Only…" His smile disappeared. "You won't tell anyone about the SantaCon thing, will you?"

"Don't worry. We won't."

Alice and Ona stood up. But Alice turned to Lewis again.

"One last thing. Wade was carrying a leather pouch—like a laptop sleeve or document portfolio—on the day he died. It might have contained documents or even photos. Any idea where it went?"

"It's gone?" Lewis asked, sounding relieved.

"Yes, it's gone."

He smiled, this time more brightly. "Good. And I hope it never turns up."

CHAPTER 12

That night at the Pemberley Inn—the old Victorian inn with a Jane Austen theme—Alice and Ona sat on Alice's four-poster canopy bed. Leaning against the hardwood headboard, the two of them, both in flannel pajamas, sipped from mugs of herbal tea.

"This is cozy," Ona said.

"And this is delicious tea," Alice said.

"Courtesy of Kendra."

Alice took another sip. Rooibos, lemongrass, lemon peel, vanilla—and some other flowery flavor.

She loved these leisurely moments with Ona.

Alice rented her room, the Colonel Brandon Suite, at a generous rate—an agreement that worked well for both of them. Alice wanted to pay for her use of the room and Ona loved that her friend lived upstairs at her inn.

"So," Ona said. "Lewis Tuttle. Killer or no?"

"He's got the motive," Alice said. "Maybe he's also got the means and opportunity: He knows about poisons and people spotted him near the trailer before Wade died. But..."

"But?"

"I just don't see it. Why did he tell us everything about the loan? He could've lied. Wade's loan wasn't legal—it was basically blackmail—so presumably he didn't keep a record of it. Lewis wouldn't tell anyone. Which means Wade would've taken the secret to his grave."

Ona said, "Wade was a real snake, wasn't he? He must've known Lewis was in financial trouble. That's why he showed up at the pharmacy and offered to give him a loan." She thought for a moment. "I guess you're right. If Lewis didn't tell anyone, then why would Wade?"

Alice nodded. "Here's another thing to consider. If Wade preyed on Lewis, maybe he preyed on others, too. The list of suspects might be long. But Wade took their names with him to the grave."

Ona took a sip of tea, a frown forming over her one visible brow.

"That leather pouch he carried around. Its contents would tell us a lot."

"If we can find it."

"Yes, if…"

They drank their tea in silence for a while. Alice considered what had happened. Her mind circled Wade and what little they knew about him so far. Her instinct told her that Lewis wasn't the killer. It also told her there was something fishy about Bunce. But was there a connection to Wade's death? And if so, what?

"We need to learn more about Wade," she said.

"Mariella will know," Ona said.

They agreed to talk to Mariella tomorrow. Then their conversation drifted away from the murder. They talked about the Christmas fair. She told Ona about the strange secret Santa gifting her customers with sequels. Then they talked about Andrea's holiday pies and all the other delicious treats they were going to indulge in tomorrow.

Outside, the wind pressed against the walls of the inn. Snow whipped against the windows. The cold was deadly outside, but in her bedroom, it was cozy and warm.

So cozy and warm that Alice could almost forget that there was a killer on the loose.

Almost.

CHAPTER 13

*I*n the morning, Alice and Ona went looking for Mariella Ridgeway.

The wind whipped through town. Few other pedestrians braved Main Street at this hour. Snow whirled around their legs and twisted into devilish shapes before rushing off. A man passed them, head down, hand clutching the top of his coat to keep the icy cold out.

Alice and Ona didn't speak. The few times Alice attempted conversation, her teeth ached with the cold. She shut her mouth and lowered her head at the oncoming wind, like a bull lowering its horns at an adversary.

Eventually, they reached the Christmas fair. The little village of stalls looked abandoned. It was early—too early for the stalls to open—but if this weather kept up, no one would want to stroll around the fair, anyway. There was no sauntering in this weather, only a constant battle to move forward, get ahead, escape the ice and snow.

Ona shouldered open the gate marked "staff only."

Inside the staff-only area, Alice squinted through the flurries at the Santa trailer. The door was shut. Locked, she knew, and there was a laminated sign pegged to the door that warned trespassers to "STAY OUT" by order of the Blithedale Police Department. Mayor MacDonald had convinced Chief Jimbo to avoid crime scene tape—no need to bring more attention to the murder, was there?

In the distance, she thought the shadowy outline of a man atop a ladder. Was someone really balancing at the top of that ladder and working on the parade floats? In this weather?

Ona pulled open the door to the trailer marked "Management & Logistics" and Alice followed her inside. It was like stepping out of a loud bar or nightclub and shutting the roaring music in. In the sudden stillness inside the trailer, she heard her own panting and felt her beating heart.

She stomped the snow off her boots and shook her coat.

Ben Ridgeway, wrapped in his bright red scarf, swiveled around on a desk chair and shot to his feet. He said, "Some weather, huh? Let me get you something warm to drink."

His mother, Mariella, was at another desk, tapping away at the keyboard with frenetic energy. Her phone rang. She had earbuds in her ear. She touched one of them and said, "Ridgeway Cleaning, Mariella Ridgeway speaking. Yes?"

The "yes" was delivered with the force of an ultimatum. She nodded, said "yes" twice, and then, "Add another cleaner to the job. We'll absorb the cost." She touched her earbud. While talking on the phone, her typing hadn't slowed one iota.

Ben brought Alice and Ona cups of coffee. The tips of Alice's fingers burned with cold, and it was a relief to wrap them around the warm cup.

"So?" Ben said. "What brings you to our HQ on a morning like this?" Then his face darkened. "Sorry. Stupid me. You're here about my dad, aren't you?"

"We have some questions for you and your mom."

Ben sighed. "Chief Jimbo called us and said you would drop by. Hey, Mom."

Mariella continued to type. "What?"

"Alice is helping Chief Jimbo and needs to ask us some questions about Dad."

"Go ahead, ask. No, wait a minute." She touched her earbud again. "Ridgeway Cleaning, Mariella Ridgeway speaking. Yes?"

Ben shrugged, an apologetic gesture, and said, "She's busy."

But a few seconds later, Mariella got to her feet. She strode to a row of hooks on the wall and grabbed a coat. As she wrestled it on, she faced Alice. "I have to go. Emergency at a client facility. Well? What did you want to ask?"

"What can you tell us about Wade?"

"That's what we call an open-ended question," she said. She glanced impatiently at her wristwatch. "All right. The 20-second version. Wade and I met after college. He was handsome back then, charming as hell, and seemed ambitious. I thought he was a good catch. He wasn't. His looks faded, his charm was pure manipulation, and his only ambition was to cut corners and make a lot of money by not working. A terrible catch." She let out a short, exasperated breath and turned to her son. "Ben, can you fill in the rest for me, please?"

Then she yanked open the trailer door, letting in a blast of wind and snow. The door slammed shut. She was gone.

Alice stared at the door, then at Ona, who shook her head.

"Look, I'm sorry," Ben said. "She's rattled. We both are. Dad's sudden death—"

Alice said, "I understand. Though what she said about him being a bad catch..."

"My mom's honest. Sometimes to a fault. She often rubs

people the wrong way, but we have clients who will stick with us, even though some competitors have lower prices, because they know she'll do right by them."

"She suggested your dad was—" Alice searched for a diplomatic word.

"Difficult," Ben said, helping her out. "Look, Mom's had to put up with my dad's stuff for many years. It wasn't easy."

"What did you think of your dad?"

He reflected on the question for a moment, then said, "He and I didn't talk much, to be honest. But I tried to give him the benefit of the doubt. In his own way, my dad struggled. He never had a purpose. Mom and I have this business, and you see how she pours her heart and soul into it. Dad had to find his own way."

"And did he?"

Ben shrugged. "For years, he'd been content to drift, but recently he'd been trying to cobble something together. And fast."

"Why?"

"You saw how straightforward my mom is. She doesn't keep her feelings secret. He saw the writing on the wall. Eventually, she was going to throw him out."

"Throw him out? The house, it's—"

"My mom's, yes. The house. The cars. The business. Everything's hers. Despite years of plans and projects—from a career in telesales to an internet business—he did nothing."

"How do you feel about that?"

He gave her a sharp look. "Are you psychoanalyzing me?"

Alice said nothing, waiting for his answer.

The door to the trailer burst open, the wind rushing in. Mohammad, shrouded in snow, stepped inside and forced the door shut behind him. He stomped his feet.

"Mr. Ridgeway—" He made a face. "—Ben. I've fixed the reindeer float, but I'm not sure it will hold in this wind. It will probably tear open again. Also, do we have a new staff sheet?"

"Sure, right over here." Ben picked up a clipboard with several sheets attached to it. "Why?"

"Mrs. Digby needs extra help with one of the stalls, and I—"

Ben hugged the clipboard to his chest. "Don't worry about it, Mohammad. You shouldn't have to deal with that. I'll handle Mrs. Digby."

Ben pulled on a parka and moved toward the door. Alice grabbed his arm before he could vanish.

"Ben, you never answered my question."

He stared at her, as if assessing her. Then his face softened. "All right. You want to know how I felt about my dad? Alienated. Frustrated. Disgusted. Mostly, I didn't care what he did. Eventually, he'd walk out of our lives, and I wouldn't miss him. But—" He held up a finger, his voice firm, decisive. "—I didn't kill him. Why bother? Soon, he would've been gone from my life, anyway."

He turned and pulled open the door.

He added, "And good riddance."

CHAPTER 14

a brisk business at Wonderland Books kept Alice busy the entire day, barely leaving her time for lunch. That evening, a small crowd gathered in the Pemberley Inn's lounge to watch *It's a Wonderful Life*. The inn's guests settled into the armchairs and couches—a couple with their teenage daughter, a group of thirty-something friends, a pair of octogenarian sisters—while Alice and Ona grabbed chairs from the kitchen and placed them near the entrance to the lounge.

A fire crackled in the fireplace. Outside the French doors, the wind howled. Snow pelted the windows, the glass panes shuddering, and an icy draft fought its way through the cracks of the old mansion, petering out in the cozy warmth from the fire.

Alice and Ona spent the beginning of the movie bringing mulled wine and cookies for the guests, but then Edie and Fleur stepped in and insisted on taking over.

"We're done for the day at the restaurant," Edie said.

"But we're not done working," Fleur added.

"So put up your feet and have some mulled wine."

Edie and Fleur, both young women with the same purple

hair, worked at Under the Greenwood Tree and lived in a room at the inn. Ona had made them a deal: So long as you help out, you can stay until you can afford a place of your own. It was typical of Ona to be so generous. But then Edie and Fleur deserved all the help they could get. They had saved Alice's life at Halloween—and done a great deal to help them all catch a spooky killer.

Alice and Ona sat down. Edie brought them each a mug of mulled wine. Fleur offered them plates of sugar cookies.

"This is nice," Alice said. "Only thing we're missing is—"

"Becca!" Ona cried out.

Becca walked into the lounge, a smile on her face.

"We didn't think you could get away from the diner," Ona said.

"I didn't either. But with the snow and wind, people are staying home, and Susan said she'd be happy to handle the last couple of hours and then close up."

Ona hurried to the kitchen and got another chair for Becca.

As soon as Becca sat down next to Alice, Edie and Fleur presented her with a mug of mulled wine and a plate of cookies. Alice leaned against Becca, putting her head on her friend's shoulder.

"So glad you're here," she said.

"Me, too."

For a while, they drank their mulled wine, nibbled their sugar cookies, and watched the classic movie with James Stewart as George Bailey.

But after a while, Becca nudged Alice. She whispered, "Tell me about the investigation."

Keeping her voice low, Alice filled her friend in on the latest, ending with the encounter with Mariella and Ben Ridgeway.

"Sounds like Mariella didn't have a moment to spare for you," Becca said, and frowned.

Ona leaned across Alice. "She looked busy. But I did wonder..."

"Considering her husband was murdered," Becca said, "you'd think she would have time to talk to you."

"Well, I'm not the police," Alice said. "Not officially, anyway."

"What about Ben Ridgeway?" Becca asked.

"Ben was honest, I think. He obviously disliked his dad, but as he himself said, he had no reason to kill him. His mom would've kicked him out soon. He would be gone from their lives."

"That's assuming he was telling us the truth," Ona cut in.

Alice frowned. She'd believed Ben. In fact, she admitted to herself, she'd wanted to believe him. She liked Ben. But Ona was right—they didn't know for a fact that Mariella planned to get rid of Wade. If he was telling the truth, though, neither Mariella nor Ben would have a motive for murder, would they? Unless...

"Wade had something on Lewis," Alice said. "What if he had something on Mariella, too?"

Ona frowned. "Like he was blackmailing her? His own wife? But why?"

"To keep her from divorcing him. After all, without Mariella, Wade would have no money."

Ona nodded. "That's a good theory."

Alice sighed. "But it's only a theory. Guesswork. We need more facts."

For a while, she stared into her mug, thinking through her next steps. Becca voiced the obvious conclusion before she could put words to it herself.

"You need to talk to Mariella again," Becca said.

Alice agreed. "Tomorrow, I'll find her. I'll corner her, if I have to."

"The offices of Ridgeway Cleaning are in Tilbury Town."

"Then that's where I'll corner her."

They put the investigation aside and focused on the film. They'd reached the finale, the scene where George was reunited with his family. A bell jingled on the Christmas tree. His little daughter said, "Look, Daddy. Teacher says every time a bell rings, an angel gets his wings," as the crowd of friends gathered in their home sang "Auld Lang Syne."

Alice's chest tightened and then the tears trickled down her cheek. She ran a sleeve across her cheeks. "Dammit, I can't help it. 'Auld Lang Syne' gets me every time."

Sheepishly, she looked at Becca and Ona.

Both of them were dabbing tears from her cheeks, too.

CHAPTER 15

*A*fter saying goodnight to her friends, Alice headed upstairs. Outside her bedroom stood a mannequin wearing a flannel waistcoat. Ona had named him Colonel Brandon, in tribute to Jane Austen's *Sense & Sensibility*. And since it was almost Christmas, Alice had added a Santa hat to his head.

"You make a handsome Santa, Colonel Brandon," she said as she opened her door. "Goodnight."

After the heat coming from the fireplace in the lounge, her room felt chilly. But then she'd forgotten to draw the curtains earlier to keep out the draft. She crossed the room to the window.

Looking out at Main Street was like looking at white noise on a TV screen. The wind threw the snow down and sideways and even sent it swirling upward. A car rolled down the street, moving so carefully she could imagine the anxious driver inside, unable to see much through the windscreen. She thought of Becca, who was driving home in this weather.

She grabbed her phone and sent Becca a message.

> Home yet?

> Home and snug as a bug. Thanks for a
> wonderful evening. XO!

If this stormy weather continued, what would happen to the fair?

She sighed. *Well, one thing's for sure: No one can deputize me to change the weather.*

She watched the snow dance outside the window, thinking that no sane person would want to go outside in this weather...when she saw not one, but two figures fighting their way through the snow.

They were bent over, heads down, to keep the snow out of their faces. Snow covered their hats and coats. One of them walked faster than the other, and the one falling behind stopped and waved his arms.

It was a man. But the light from a nearby streetlamp was dim and his face was half-covered by a snow-crusted scarf. She couldn't make out his identity. As he shouted against the wind, however, his scarf dropped and she recognized him.

"Bunce," she muttered to herself. "What are you doing out in this weather?"

And who was his companion?

The other person stopped. Bunce caught up, and the two of them struggled on down Main Street.

Alice wondered where they were going on a night like this.

Only one way to find out...

She grabbed her phone and shot off a message to Ona.

> You awake?

> Yup.

> Go for a walk?

You're kidding.

A couple minutes later, they were in their winter books and coats, hurrying down the inn's porch steps. They passed the statue of Old Mayor Townsend, a heavy layer of snow covering his head and shoulders.

Down the street, in the opposite direction from where Bunce and his companion had gone, a tow truck was hitching up an old, rusty pickup. Words stenciled on the side had flaked off, but part of it was still legible: "Nursery."

"Look," Alice shouted over the howling wind.

Ona's head bobbed. Her eyepatch with its rhinestones glittered under the streetlight.

"I bet their pickup broke down," she yelled at Ona. "They're hoofing it."

"But going where?"

"I have an idea."

Ona raised a gloved hand and gave her a thumbs up.

Bunce and his companion had a head start, and they might be long gone by now. But if that was their pickup being towed, why not hitch a ride with the driver?

Whatever they came for must be important. Important enough to brave this weather and leave their broke-down pickup behind.

She and Ona battled the wind and swirls of snow. It was slow going. Alice felt as if she were climbing a mountain and the mountain top kept moving farther and farther away. Drifts of snow, cast up by a snowplow, blocked parts of the sidewalk, and they had to scramble over it. Alice fell. Ona tried to help her up, and fell, too. Alice would've laughed, if she hadn't been so cold and impatient to catch Bunce.

Finally, they reached the Christmas fair. The passages between the stalls offered a little more cover than Main

Street's open wind tunnel, and it was a relief to suddenly move more swiftly over the thick blanket of snow.

"They're here," Alice said, and Ona squinted her one visible eye at her, clearly not hearing a thing over the screeching wind. So Alice pointed.

The gate next to the stage stood open.

As they moved out from the passage between the stalls and onto the spectator space in front of the stage, it unnerved Alice how much the enormous Christmas tree was bending. Then the wind dove and whipped around her and Ona, like some fierce animal that was glad to have found them again. They battled on past the gate.

The "Management & Logistics" trailer, which Alice had assumed Bunce was interested in, was dark. The door was shut. Alice tried the handle. It didn't budge. Locked.

Then where did Bunce and the other person go...?

Ona tugged at her sleeve, and she turned. Ona was pointing across the path to the other trailer. Light spilled out from beneath the door. Someone was inside the trailer for "Santa Claus Contestants." The crime scene.

Ona leaned close and cupped her hands around Alice's left ear.

"Should we interrupt them?"

Alice shook her head.

"Watch what they do?" Ona said. "Then stop them?"

Alice raised a thumb.

But they couldn't stand outside the trailer. They needed to hide and watch from a distance. Once Bunce and his friend came out, they could follow them—and hopefully learn what they'd been doing at the crime scene.

Alice looked around. Down the passage between the trailers stood the cluster of Christmas parade floats, with Rudolph at the front. Deep shadows between the floats made it a convenient place to hide.

Alice grabbed Ona by the hand and led her toward the hiding place. The wind tugged at the floats, their material rippling and groaning. The elf that Mohammad and Ben had fixed was taking another beating. Its arm was coming apart at the seams again, swinging ominously in the gusts of wind. They crouched down beneath the towering reindeer, which nodded its head at them.

The wind drowned out everything. They had no prospect of eavesdropping on Bunce and his friend. But on the flip side, Alice and Ona also didn't risk making too much noise and revealing their presence. They'd have to make a real racket to draw anyone's attention.

They waited. Ona leaned close and cupped her hand over Alice's ear again.

"What are they doing?"

Alice shook her head. "Stealing evidence?"

"Bunce? A killer?"

Ona pulled back and shook her head.

Alice knew what she meant. She'd never liked Bunce—he was a mean-spirited, crotchety, old Scrooge—but why would he have killed Wade Ridgeway?

A gust of wind whipped at them, buffeting Alice. She grabbed hold of Ona to steady herself. Behind her, something ripped.

Up ahead, the trailer door flew open and Bunce and the other man—it was a man, but who?—staggered out into the storm. They slammed the door shut.

Then the wind seemed to double back and drive into Alice and Ona from the other direction, battering them with snow. Something groaned—then screeched—and a drawn-out rip sent chills down her spine, as if someone had stuffed snow down her back.

She cringed.

Then a blunt object whacked her. It threw her forward,

and she screamed, rolling over in the deep snow, trying to get away from her attacker.

A third man? How many accomplices did Bunce have?

But as she scrambled to her feet, she realized an object, not a person, had clobbered her. One of the floats. The elf? Its arm must've come loose again.

No, it was Rudolph.

The wind had torn the sculpture's head off, and as it swung down, it had clubbed her. Only a few wires kept the reindeer head attached to the body. It swung in the wind.

"Alice!" Ona yelled, grabbing her by the arm and hauling her to her feet. "You OK?"

Other voices were yelling, too.

Alice turned and saw Bunce and his friend running through the open gate.

"They heard us," Ona yelled. "They saw us."

"Stop them!" Alice yelled back.

They struggled against the wind. Running in the snow was like running on a sand beach, slow and hard, sending shooting pains up Alice's thighs.

They passed through the gate and hurried down the passage between the stalls.

Out on Main Street, she was sure she and Ona could catch up with the two men. But as they clomped out of the fairgrounds, the lights of a car pulled away from the curb. A sign glowed on its roof: TAXI.

Alice caught a last glimpse of Bunce through the back window.

Then the taxi glided down Main Street, vanishing into the wall of white flurries.

CHAPTER 16

"*I* can't believe Bunce and his friend broke into a crime scene," Alice said for the umpteenth time the next morning. "And then got away."

Ona swung the steering wheel, and the pickup bumped off the street in Tilbury Town and into the parking lot by an office building. A giant blue sign on the side of the office building said, "Ridgeway Cleaning." She pulled into a space and cut the engine.

Ona turned to Alice. "We could ask Chief Jimbo to haul Bunce in for tampering with evidence."

"He'd clam up. Besides, I went to the trailer earlier this morning."

"And?"

"And I can't see that anything's missing. The most important evidence—the thermoses, the cups—that's all with Lenny Stout, anyway."

"Then what was Bunce doing in that trailer?"

"And who was he with? That's the first thing we need to work out."

"Correction," Ona said, opening her door. "The first thing we need to do is talk to Mariella Ridgeway."

Overhead, the sky was clear, the air icy cold. Banks of snow flanked the roads, and on their way to Tilbury Town from Blithedale, Alice had spotted plows grinding snow up into drifts, people shoveling their driveways, and cars half buried under mounds of white.

Leaving the pickup behind, Alice and Ona hurried across the parking lot. They walked through a set of glass doors and into a spotless reception, where a woman greeted them with a big smile.

"Welcome to Ridgeway Cleaning. How may I help?"

"We're here to see Mariella Ridgeway," Alice said.

"Do you have an appointment?"

"No, but—"

The receptionist looked sad as she clicked away at her keyboard and glanced at a screen.

"Oh, I'm so sorry. I'm afraid she's in meetings all day. But if you'd like to leave your name and number, I'll contact you about scheduling a meeting."

Alice's heart fell. Another setback. "Is there any chance she can see us? It's important…"

"I'm very sorry. Mrs. Ridgeway—"

"Maybe I can help," a voice said behind them.

Alice turned. Mohammad, the Ridgeway Cleaning employee who'd been working at the Christmas fair, approached the reception. Leaning against the counter, he spoke with the receptionist, picked up a stack of mail for Mariella Ridgeway, and then said to Alice and Ona, "Mrs. Ridgeway really is in meetings all day. In fact, she's visiting clients, so she's not even at the office today. But maybe I can answer your questions. Come, please."

He gestured toward a door that stood open nearby. Alice and Ona exchanged looks, then followed him into the small meeting room. He encouraged them to sit at the conference table that dominated the room. There was a large flatscreen on one wall. Another held a whiteboard.

"Coffee? Tea? Water?" Mohammad smiled. "What can I get you? Our coffee is excellent. I promise."

Alice relented and asked for coffee. So did Ona.

Mohammad left the room.

Alice sighed. "We're getting nowhere."

"Don't be so sure of that."

Ona pushed herself up in her seat and craned her neck to look at the pile of letters Mohammad had left on the table. Alice followed her gaze. The top letter was from a law firm.

Before Alice could ask about it, Ona sank back into her seat.

Mohammad was returning, carrying two cups of coffee. "Two Americanos."

He sat down without a coffee of his own.

"So," he said. "How can I help?"

Alice sipped her coffee, which turned out to be excellent. Creamy on top, earthy and strong underneath. She said, "We need to talk to Mrs. Ridgeway about her husband's death."

Mohammad frowned and shook his head. "Horrible. Shocking."

"Is everyone shocked by what happened?"

"Of course we are."

His eyes drifted to the side. It was only for an instant, then his focus returned to Alice and Ona.

"But?" Alice prodded.

Mohammad shifted in his chair. He put his hands on the table. Then pulled them back and placed them in his lap, suddenly uncomfortable.

"Mohammad," Alice said, leaning forward in her chair. "We're investigating a murder. Even if people didn't like Wade, murder is murder."

Mohammad nodded. "Yes, I was shocked," he said. Then sighed. "But not surprised."

"It didn't surprise you Wade Ridgeway died?"

"This has nothing to do with Ridgeway Cleaning. Do we agree?"

"All right," Alice said. Mohammad looked at Ona, too, and Ona said, "Sure."

"Ridgeway Cleaning has been good to me," Mohammad said. "Mrs. Ridgeway has been good to me. When war broke out in my country, my wife and I fled to the U.S. with our children. I needed work. But it's hard to find work that can feed a family. Most cleaning companies pay their people next to nothing. But Ridgeway Cleaning is different."

"Different how?"

"We get paid a decent wage. My wife and I make enough money to feed our family, put aside savings for a house one day, and college for our kids. That's all because Mrs. Ridgeway believes cleaners should be paid a fair wage for their work."

Alice and Ona both nodded.

Mohammad continued: "I worked hard. Mrs. Ridgeway paid for language classes, so I, and others like me, could speak better English. She gave me a promotion. Now I'm a cleaning manager with my own team."

He smiled, obviously proud of his achievement.

"None of it would be possible without Mrs. Ridgeway," he said. "She is an angel."

"But her husband?"

Mohammad made a face. "A bad man."

"Bad in what way?"

"He acted like he was the boss. He would tell me what to do. Once, he even asked me to do work for someone who wasn't an official client. He wanted me to clean the man's offices and then the man would pay Mr. Ridgeway. In cash, of course."

"Did he get away with it?"

Mohammad shook his head. "It was against our code of conduct, which we take very seriously. So I reported it to Mrs. Ridgeway. She thanked me. She was very mad at her husband. They were in her office when I heard her tell him never to do that again. He yelled at her." He looked embarrassed. "I don't eavesdrop. Not normally. But I stayed outside the door. I worried he would hurt her."

"Was he a violent man?"

"He yelled. He called her names. Ugly names. But he didn't hit her, if that's what you mean. She told him to keep his hands off her business. After that, Mr. Ridgeway never tried that kind of thing again—at least with me." His face darkened. "I'm sure he stole money from her, though. I'm sure of it."

After their conversation ended, Alice and Ona returned to the pickup truck. Alice admitted the trip wasn't a complete waste of time.

She said, "So Wade was stealing. Would that be enough of a motive for Mariella to murder him, though? On the other hand, what if he was blackmailing her into staying married?"

"He wasn't," Ona said. "Or if he was, I bet she didn't care."

"Oh?"

"That letter from a law firm? That was an invoice. And I've heard of the law firm. They're Tilbury Town's top divorce lawyers." Ona turned the key in the ignition and warm air blasted from the heaters. "I bet Mariella was weeks —or maybe only days—away from kicking her husband out and divorcing him."

I bet. I guess.

Until they could corner Mariella herself, Alice reflected, it was all speculation.

CHAPTER 17

*B*ack in Blithedale, Alice opened Wonderland Books in time to let Mr. and Mrs. Oriel inside. The Oriels were an older couple who, in their matching glasses and clothes, looked oddly identical. Alice liked them —if all couples were as compatible, the world would be a better place.

"Looking for something in particular?" she asked.

Mrs. Oriel put a hand on her arm and leaned close, speaking in a confidential tone. "I'm looking for something dark and stormy."

"You mean like a gothic novel?"

Mr. Oriel jumped in. "She means something hot and spicy."

"A romance?"

They both nodded.

Mrs. Oriel said, "We've been reading Clyde Digby's books, and let me tell you—"

"They may not leave you with lingering intellectual questions…" Mr. Oriel said.

"But they keep the bed warm," Mrs. Oriel said with a wink.

Mr. Oriel nodded, a boyish grin on his face, and suddenly didn't know where to put his hands. He settled on shoving them into his pockets.

"Well, all right," Alice said, and after a few minutes of looking through her selection of romance novels with the Oriels, sent the couple out into the frigid weather with a bagful of hot novels.

Alice loved the thousands of ways that books affected people. Stories made them happy, and sad, and curious—and, yes, even aroused.

And cozy, too, of course.

After last night's adventures and this morning's visit to Tilbury Town, she was glad to be back among her books. Some people needed alcohol or a particular blanket or bathrobe for comfort, but for her, nothing could beat a room full of books.

She restocked her shelves and sorted through more donations. There were fewer in the box today, no doubt because of the stormy weather yesterday. She flipped through books, dipping into the texts, reading a page and savoring the words, then sampling another story.

She picked up a collection of Christmas poems and read one by Christina Rossetti that began,

> In the bleak midwinter, frosty wind made moan,
> Earth stood hard as iron, water like a stone;
> Snow had fallen, snow on snow, snow on snow,
> In the bleak midwinter, long ago.

The door opened, and Alice replaced the book. A young woman came into the store, and as she pulled off her winter hat and her black curls emerged, Alice recognized her as

Kendra Digby. Behind her came Ben Ridgeway in his red scarf.

"Alice, I'm looking for a book…"

"Don't tell me it's the first book in a series."

Kendra gave her a mystified look. "No, it's Paulo Coelho's *The Alchemist*. I usually have a few copies at my store, but I'm sold out, and we're reading it in my spirituality book club."

Alice confirmed she had a copy of *The Alchemist*.

"Do you have a second copy?" Kendra asked. "Ben hasn't read it."

Ben smiled. "That's all right. I'm not really into all that woo-woo stuff."

Kendra turned sharply, a wounded look passing over her face. But she hid it a moment later by swatting his arm and laughing. "You're being beastly, as usual."

"Beastly Ben, that's me," he said, grinning.

Kendra paid for the book, and the two of them opened the door again. As they hurried out, letting in a blast of icy air, a tall, gangly figure strode inside. It was Todd Townsend. He shut the door and stomped the snow from his boots. Then unwrapped himself, plucking the hat from his head and unwinding his scarf.

Finally, he reached inside his coat and drew out a book. He slapped it down on the counter.

Elena Ferrante's *The Story of a New Name*.

"This book is not my kind of book," Todd said, sounding offended. Then he let out an exasperated sigh. "So, why the heck did I get hooked after page one? And why is this book number two in the series and not book one? Now I need to stop reading and go back and start from the beginning."

He said all this as if accusing Alice herself of some grievous injustice.

"Someone left the damn book in my mailbox."

Alice's reaction was simply to stare.

"That's right," Todd said, misinterpreting her reaction. "Someone left me the second book in a series in my mailbox during one of the worst winter storms in recent memory. Can you believe it?"

"Yes, I can."

As she found a copy of the first book in Elena Ferrante's Neapolitan Quartet, *My Brilliant Friend*, she told Todd about the other people who had received similarly puzzling gifts in their mailboxes.

He looked thoughtful. "Always sequels, huh? This will be good for my readership. No one can resist a secret Santa story. Of course, murder is always better."

Alice gave him a reproachful look.

Todd shrugged and said, "It's the truth. People say they hate reading about murder, but then they can't resist clicking on that headline."

He paid for the book. "So, tell me, any progress on the investigation?"

Alice would have to be careful not to share too much with Todd or it would end up on *The Blithedale Record*'s website with a sensational headline at the top. She could share the full details later during the "exclusive interview" Mayor MacDonald had promised him.

"I'm trying to find Bunce," she said.

"Good luck. I thought I'd see him around the Christmas fair in his Santa costume, but for a guy who wants to win the Santa contest, he isn't working the crowds very much. You think he's connected to the murder?"

Alice ignored the question. "I've seen him. He was with another guy."

Todd gave her a wry smile. "That's very specific, Alice."

She thought of the man who'd joined Bunce in breaking into the trailer. She'd seen so little of him, he might be anyone. Then she thought of the pickup truck being towed.

"He drives a pickup truck from a nursery."

"A plant nursery? Well, lots of people work at plant nurseries…"

Yet Todd was smiling, clearly enjoying that he knew something she didn't.

"Why are you so interested in this guy who works at a plant nursery?"

"I told you," Alice said, crossing her arms on her chest. "I saw him with Bunce."

They stared each other down.

Finally, Todd waved the book and said, "Just because I'm feeling impatient to get back to my reading, I'll tell you. Besides, I expect all the details during our interview." He winked. "Vickers. He owns a plant nursery in Tilbury Town."

"Vickers? The guy who was hired to run the Santa contest?"

"Hired?" Todd shook his head. "No, no, he wasn't hired. He's a volunteer, like everyone else. And very generous of him, too, don't you think?"

His sarcasm was inescapable.

Alice said, "You don't think Vickers is much of a charitable guy?"

"You go talk to him and see what you think. But as for me,"—he pulled on his hat and scarf again and zipped up his coat—"I think he's about as charitable as Wade Ridgeway."

CHAPTER 18

hat evening, Alice met Becca and Ona for dinner at the What the Dickens Diner. Alice and Ona sat at the counter. Becca ate in between work, occasionally slipping away to help Susan with customers.

Outside, the temperature had plummeted. Becca's special of the day was a beef-and-lentil soup with chopped tomatoes and plenty of hearty vegetables: carrots, peppers, celery, cabbage, and spinach. It was exactly what Alice needed—food that warmed her from within.

As she dipped hunks of sourdough bread into the soup, she shared the latest news. Becca had already heard about their late-night experience at the Christmas fair, and now Alice could tell both her and Ona who the mystery man was: Vickers.

"Todd is skeptical about Vickers' motivation for volunteering," she said.

"I don't know Vickers well," Becca said. "But I've met him, and Todd is right—he's no Santa. He seems more likely to win an award for Grinch impersonator of the year."

"Like Bunce."

"They're a fine pair, yes. But one possibility is that Vickers is volunteering so he can advertise for his nursery. The Christmas fair is also an opportunity to network with other business owners."

Becca had a point. There might be non-charitable reasons that people volunteered. Mariella Ridgeway wasn't simply investing money and contributing staff out of the goodness of her own heart—it was great exposure for Ridgeway Cleaning.

"Still, the two of them broke into a crime scene," Ona said. "Something fishy's going on."

Lenny Stout slipped onto a stool next to Alice. "Something fishy is definitely going on," he agreed. "Unless you call aconite poisoning your everyday method of murder."

"I'm guessing I shouldn't," Alice said uncertainly. "What's aconite?"

"An extract from a highly poisonous plant. Also called monkshood. That's what was in Wade's cup. That's what killed him."

Alice brought out her phone and opened the browser.

"What's up, Alice?" Ona asked, leaning close.

Alice searched for plant nurseries in Tilbury Town. She found the right one: Vickers & Vickers' Plant Nursery. She clicked on the link. Then scrolled through the site.

She held up the phone for Lenny to see. "Is that the one?"

Lenny squinted at the phone. Then nodded. "That's the one."

She'd shown him a sales page with information about monkshood. Vickers sold the plant at his nursery.

"Probably lots of plant nurseries sell it," Lenny said. "People grow it in their gardens. Though no garden around here will have a flowering aconite right now, of course." He gestured toward the snow-covered town outside. "But if you really want to get your hands on aconite, you can order it online. It's even used in some alternative medicines."

"We need to talk to Vickers," Alice told Becca and Ona. Then she turned back to Lenny. "Did the thermos or cup reveal anything else?"

Lenny shrugged. "It's what they didn't reveal that's interesting. The poison was only in Wade's cup—not the thermos. Not a trace of it anywhere else."

"Which means?" Ona asked.

"Which means," Alice said, "that the killer targeted Wade but didn't want to risk someone else drinking the deadly hot chocolate. The killer didn't want anyone else to die."

"That is interesting. Any fingerprints?"

Lenny shook his head. "Wade's on the cup and the thermos, but nobody else's."

"And what about the Santa bag that was found next to him?"

"Chief Jimbo was supposed to run fingerprints on the rest of the trailer. I only did the cup and thermos since I was dealing with toxicology. You'd better talk to Chief Jimbo."

Alice nodded.

The night after Bunce and Vickers had broken into the trailer, she'd gone back to check to see what was missing. She'd assumed several items were in Lenny's possession, being tested for fingerprints and toxins at the lab. Which was why she hadn't looked for the Santa bag. Now she couldn't remember seeing it in the trailer.

Had Bunce and Vickers broken in to steal the Santa bag?

CHAPTER 19

a sign clung to the wire fence: "Vickers & Vickers' Plant Nursery." One side of the sign had come loose, and it dangled precariously.

Ona's pickup rumbled into the yard. The wheels banged into potholes, jolting Alice in her seat. She gazed out the window. Snow-covered planters stood in rows. A metal rack held a few plastic and ceramic pots, but it looked picked over, badly in need of new stock.

Ona parked the pickup. "So this is it, huh? Vickers' business empire."

"It's seen better days."

"No kidding."

They got out of the pickup. Alice tugged her coat close to her throat. Overnight, clouds had rolled in and covered the blue sky again. The icy wind was back. The forecast promised more snow.

The property comprised the wide, snow-covered yard and a low, aluminum-sided building. Beyond it, at the top of a low rise near the back of the property, stood a single-story house.

"There's the pickup," Ona said.

"That's the one," Alice agreed.

The tow truck must've dumped it here. Maybe Vickers wasn't willing—or able—to pay for a mechanic to fix it. The truck stood near the main nursery building, its paint chipped, rust eating the body from the bottom up. If she'd seen it in a junkyard, Alice would've assumed it had stopped running years ago.

Not a reliable vehicle for a getaway, she thought, imagining how frustrated Vickers and Bunce must've been when the truck broke down in Blithedale the other night. But they'd been clever enough to order a cab in time for a quick exit.

Inside the main building, the nursery looked no less run down. Fluorescent lamps cast a sickly light over the store, some of them flickering, one dead. Metal shelves stood empty. Plants drooped. Boxes contained half their capacity of seed packets. An empty section marked "watering cans" bore a handwritten sign that said, "out of stock."

"Business is obviously booming," Alice muttered.

"Obviously. I'm guessing their slogan is *'We're out of stock.'*"

Ona gestured toward the back. An open doorway led to an office. Alice would've loved to snoop around, but next to the doorway stood a counter, and behind that counter sat a kid. He must've been in his teens. His face, dappled with angry red spots, drooped with boredom as he stared at his phone. Tinny screams emitted from the phone. It seemed he was watching a horror film.

"Can I help you?" he said flatly without looking up.

Alice nodded toward the office, and Ona understood. She sidled up to the counter. "What's that you're watching? Oh, is that *Saw*? I love the *Saw* movies."

Alice suppressed a laugh. *Liar. Your threshold for horror is Wuthering Heights.*

But within a few moments, Ona had drawn the kid into a

conversation about slasher movies that worked like magic, gradually erasing the boredom and replacing it with the passionate dialog of a dedicated fan.

"Yeah, yeah," the kid said. "But *Saw III* is really the masterpiece..."

Alice ducked past the counter, slipping into the office.

Ordinary interior: A window at the back, blinds down. On a desk sat a computer, keyboard, and screen. A bookshelf stood against the right-hand wall. Off to the left was a small table with a computer printer. The only decoration was a poster showing an airbrushed pinup: a naked woman draped across a vicious-looking dragon.

With "art" like this, she thought, *Vickers should be running an auto repair shop, not a plant nursery.*

The place was in disarray. Papers, including lots of unopened mail, covered the desk. The letters looked like bills. The top envelope had a red stamp on it that said, "FINAL NOTICE."

A framed photo on the desk showed a much younger Vickers standing next to an older, grizzled man. The family resemblance was strong. It must be his father. Vickers Senior. Judging by how young Vickers looked in the photo, she guessed he'd inherited the nursery some time ago. And judging by the state of the shelves and the overdue bills, he hadn't run the business with much success.

She looked beyond the desk. Oddly, a bunch of boxes lay piled up in a corner by a potted plant—its leaves brown and curling, half dead—as if they'd been tossed there.

She moved closer. They were all smartphone boxes. She picked one up. It was a leading brand—the same phone she owned, in fact—but as she turned over the box and studied the back, something about the pixelated design made her wonder. She read the fine print and noticed that the text had an error in it. Instead of "Designed in California," it said,

"Designated in California." It was a minor mistake, but she knew you'd never find such a typo on an authentic smartphone box.

They're fakes, she thought.

She put down the box and was about to look elsewhere for clues when she caught sight of something tucked behind the potted plant. She crouched down. Something made of leather...

She reached in and tugged at it. Then pulled it out. And nearly gasped when she saw what it was. A leather pouch.

Wade's missing case...

Just then Ona's voice—which had been steadily droning on about slasher films—rose in pitch. She said, "Oh, look at the time. It's time to go."

Someone was coming. Alice grabbed the leather pouch and shoved it back, hiding it again. Just as she stood back up, she heard Ona emit an unnaturally cheerful, "Oh, hi!"

Vickers stepped into the office, a frown on his face. "What the hell are you doing here?"

Alice had to think fast. She could confront him about the leather pouch, but she had no real authority. If Vickers was the killer, how could she stop him? How could she make sure that evidence didn't disappear? She needed to get professionals—real cops—involved in this, and fast.

Until then, she thought, *distract him, talk about something innocuous, something he'll think is a natural, safe topic of conversation.*

She tried to put on her best smile. She said, "Just in the neighborhood. I dropped in to ask you about the Santa contest. See, I'm writing an opinion piece for *The Blithedale Record* on the Christmas fair and wanted to learn more about the contest."

Vickers' frown deepened and his eyes narrowed. "Why? The contest is just a contest. Nothing special about it."

"Except it is special," she said. "It captures the spirit of Christmas, doesn't it? Identifying the Santa who most deserves to be celebrated for his or her generosity…"

He stared at her. His frown was approaching a glare. He balled his hands into fists.

"What are you implying?"

"I'm not implying anything."

She was confused. How had her distraction backfired so badly? What did she say to offend him?

He moved forward and grabbed her by the arm. Hard. He hissed at her, "I want you out of here and off my private property before I—before I—"

He hauled her out of the office.

Before what, she wanted to say, *you call the cops?*

But she had the feeling he'd been thinking of a different threat.

CHAPTER 20

 few hours later, Alice sat in Chief Jimbo's cruiser across the street from Vickers & Vickers' Plant Nursery in Tilbury Town. The chief of police, his nose red and raw from blowing his nose too many times, sipped from a travel mug. A rich scent of ginger and flowers and something bitter wafted over to Alice.

"Kendra's tea for the flu," Chief Jimbo explained. "It works wonders."

"You do sound better."

"I feel great." He smiled. "I've got a feeling this is it—we're about to catch the killer."

It was amazing, she reflected, how quickly Chief Jimbo had recovered once she presented the facts to him—at least enough of them to suggest that Vickers might be hiding Wade's missing leather pouch.

He does love it when a case closes.

But Alice struggled between high hopes and anxiety. High hopes that this might, in fact, be the end of the investigation. And anxiety that they'd come too late. In the time it had taken her to talk to Chief Jimbo and then for him to coordinate with the Tilbury County Sheriff's Department, Vickers could easily have disposed of any evidence.

She reflected on why Vickers and Bunce had broken into the crime scene and her conversation about fingerprints with Lenny Stout.

She said, "Chief Jimbo, you're running fingerprints on the Santa bag we found at the scene of the crime, right?"

"The Santa bag? No, I didn't think that one was relevant."

She gave him a sharp look. "What? Why not?"

"Well, the Santa contest has nothing to do with Wade. It's Vickers' responsibility."

"But what if the killer handled the bag? It was sitting right next to Wade."

Chief Jimbo's cheeks colored. "Guess you're right," he muttered. "I'll pick it up later today and run fingerprints…"

Alice groaned. She knew at once that Chief Jimbo wouldn't find a Santa bag. Bunce and Vickers must've taken it. But what else did they take? Maybe the leather pouch had been hidden within the trailer. It wouldn't take much for Chief Jimbo to miss a concealed object, since he didn't bother to deal with the ones in plain sight.

Maybe it'll turn up now, she thought, *when Chief Jimbo and Sheriff Cutter inspect Vickers' office.*

"Here's the sheriff," Chief Jimbo said.

A sheriff's cruiser pulled up to them. Chief Jimbo rolled down the window.

"Sheriff Cutter," he said.

"Jimbo," the other man said.

Sheriff Carl Cutter had a large, ruddy face with a walrus mustache and a pair of dark, beady eyes. He stared at Jimbo with poorly concealed disgust. Then noticed Alice. "What's your lady friend doing here?"

"This is Alice Hartford," Chief Jimbo said. "She runs

Wonderland Books in Blithedale, and she's helping me with the investigation."

"Helping?" Sheriff Cutter's eyes flashed. "This woman—this civilian—is *helping* you?"

The way he uttered the word *woman* made Alice think her biggest misdeed was belonging to her gender. She knew at once that she and Sheriff Cutter would not get along.

"She's kind of like a special consultant," Chief Jimbo muttered, eyes downcast.

"Good grief," Sheriff Cutter said. "Let's go talk to Mr. Vickers."

The sheriff swung his cruiser across the street and pulled into the nursery's yard. Chief Jimbo put his car in drive and followed. A moment later, they'd all left the cars and hurried into the low building.

The teenager barely reacted to their approach. He jabbed a thumb toward the office door, which was closed.

"Boss is back there."

Sheriff Cutter knocked on the door. His hand was giant and thick, the knocks as loud as a sledgehammer.

"Stop that racket and come in," a muffled voice shouted.

Sheriff Cutter threw open the door and lumbered inside.

"Mr. Vickers?"

Vickers sat behind his desk, leaning back in his chair with his hands behind his head. "You must be a cop," he sneered. "How else could you work out who I was?"

Sheriff Cutter ignored the jibe. He introduced himself and Chief Jimbo, pointedly leaving Alice out. "Mind if we ask you some questions, Mr. Vickers?"

"Go ahead and ask."

"And mind if we look around?"

"You looking for plants for your office?"

Sheriff Cutter glared at Vickers. Vickers smirked. "Go ahead. Knock yourself out."

As Sheriff Cutter moved toward the shelves along the right-hand wall, Chief Jimbo stepped inside, too. Alice followed. She glanced over at the corner and her heart sank. The helter-skelter pile of boxes with counterfeit smartphones was gone. As she'd feared, Vickers had used the time to clean up.

Sheriff Cutter said, "Mr. Vickers, did you know Wade Ridgeway?"

Vickers frowned, the hollows around his eyes growing deeper, and dropped his hands from the back of his head. "Sure, I knew him. Not well. But I knew him. Why?"

"I'll ask the questions. Where were you at the time of his death?"

Vickers looked at the sheriff. Then at Chief Jimbo. "This is about Wade's death?"

Chief Jimbo said, "Mr. Vickers, Wade had this pouch with him. Made of leather. For documents and stuff. Have you seen that anywhere?"

Sheriff Cutter glared at Jimbo, apparently displeased that the Blithedale chief of police was choosing to ask questions. But he then turned to Vickers and said, "Well, have you?"

Vickers rubbed a hand across his chin. "Let me think. I'm pretty sure I saw Wade carry a pouch around..."

While the sheriff and chief of police focused on Vickers— and he focused on them—Alice crept around the room, inching closer and closer to where the fake smartphones had been piled. The potted plant still stood in place. Balled-up pieces of paper lay on the floor. A plastic bag sat in a corner, apparently full of discarded candy bar wrappers. And there—

She darted forward. Crouched down. Grabbed the leather pouch and pulled it out.

"Here it is," she said, holding it up for the two lawmen to see.

Sheriff Cutter strode toward her and yanked the case out of her hands.

"Don't touch evidence," he snapped. Then, gripping it firmly with both of his walrus-sized paws, he confronted Vickers. "Vickers, what is this?"

"I don't—" Vickers' eyes had gone wide. "I haven't—it's not mine."

"That's right, Mr. Vickers. This isn't yours. It's Wade Ridgeway's."

Vickers' face paled. "Now, hold on a minute, I'm sure I can explain..."

Sheriff Cutter grabbed the flap on the leather pouch, undoing the clasp and flipping it open.

"Then can you explain why the pouch contains..."

He opened it wide. His eyes narrowed. His walrus mustache drooped into a frown.

"...nothing."

Alice leaned close. So did Chief Jimbo.

The leather pouch was empty.

CHAPTER 21

a downhearted Chief Jimbo dropped Alice off at the bookstore and drove on to the police department, followed closely by Sheriff Cutter in his cruiser. The sheriff had insisted he and Jimbo meet to discuss the case—"without civilians present."

Never mind, Alice told herself. *I've got a business to run.*

She'd left Wonderland Books closed for several hours of regular business already, and as she arrived, a mom and her adolescent daughter stood waiting by the front door to the bookstore. Alice apologized for making them wait out in the cold as she fumbled with her keys.

Inside the bookstore, the girl told her she would've waited the whole day, if necessary.

"Someone gave me this book as a present." She held out a copy of *Gathering Blue* by Lois Lowry. "It's the best book I've read in my entire life. But my mom says there's another book…"

"*The Giver,*" Alice said. "That's the first book in that series and—" She cut herself off. She was going to say, *And it's great.*

But there was something else she wanted to say: "Did a friend give you this book?"

"No, it's so weird," the girl said, glancing at her mom, who nodded. "Someone left it in our mailbox. The person wrapped it like a Christmas present and it had my name on a tag."

The mom added, "But not the name of the person who gave it."

"A secret Santa," Alice said. "You're not the first person to get an anonymous present this Christmas."

"I'm not?" the girl said.

Alice explained how others had come into the store asking for the first books in series after receiving sequels from a mysterious benefactor.

"It really is like Santa," the mom said.

"Mom," the girl said, giving her mom an impatient look. "We're both too old to believe in Santa."

But her eyes lit up when Alice brought her a copy of *The Giver*, and on their way out the door, the girl said, "I don't think it could be Uncle Max who sent it, do you? What about Harriet's grandma—she's always giving stuff to people…"

Alice smiled. Whoever was gifting these books was bringing people a lot of joy—and providing her with more business.

She went outside and emptied the donation box. It was half full already. Among the books were classics by Mark Twain and the Brontë sisters, as well as four books in a Regency romance series called Pennyroyal Green by Julie Anne Long.

She brought the books inside and sorted through them, adding prices.

This is wonderful, she told herself. *Let the police handle the crimes and let me handle the books.*

As she shelved books, she tried to imagine Chief Jimbo and Sheriff Cutter in conversation. What did they make of Vickers and the leather pouch? It was damning evidence, even if it was empty. Still, why would Vickers remove the contents but leave the pouch hidden in his office? It made no sense.

She was mulling this over when Mayor MacDonald stormed into the bookstore.

"Alice," he snapped. "You're supposed to be in charge of the investigation. Why is Sheriff Cutter involved?"

Alice put her hands on her hips. "Hold on a minute, mayor. I'm not supposed to lead anything. I'm not the one you appointed chief of police. Chief Jimbo is."

"But you were supposed to keep an eye on him."

"I was supposed to help him, remember?"

Mayor MacDonald waved the idea away, the way someone swats at a fly. "You've made a real mess of things now."

"I have? How have I made a mess of things?"

"Come along," he said.

Alice gestured at her bookstore. "In case you haven't noticed, I have a business to run."

"If we do nothing, you won't have a business for much longer—none of us will."

"What are you talking about?"

Three minutes later, she was sitting in the passenger seat of his SUV. He gripped the steering wheel hard, his knuckles turning white, as he drove down Main Street. He hit the brakes, and the car jerked to a stop.

"Look," he said.

He'd pulled up to the curb by the Christmas fair. The stalls were open for business and, thanks to the calmer weather, plenty of people were already milling around. But so were uniformed officers. She recognized the uniforms as belonging to the county sheriff's office.

"Sheriff Cutter's crew," Mayor MacDonald confirmed. "Who gave them permission to invade our Christmas fair? That's what I'd like to ask Chief Jimbo. But is he at his desk? No."

Mayor MacDonald put the car into drive and jerked the steering wheel to the left, pulling them away from the curb. He sped up, flying down Main Street. Then turned off. As they drove, he asked Alice about what happened, and she told him about Vickers and her visit to Tilbury Town with Chief Jimbo.

"And Sheriff Cutter," Mayor MacDonald said.

"Yes, and Sheriff Cutter."

"That man's as sticky as flypaper. We'll never get rid of him now."

Soon they were heading away from the center of town and into the neighborhood of ranch-style homes they'd visited only a few days ago.

The SUV stopped in front of Chief Jimbo's house.

Mayor MacDonald and Alice both got out, and a moment later, he was knocking on the front door. No answer.

There was a letter slot in the door. Mayor MacDonald leaned down and pushed it open. "Open the door, Jimbo," Mayor MacDonald yelled through the slot.

Still no answer.

"I'll fire you if you don't open this door."

Mayor MacDonald, his anger clearly rising, straightened up and stomped a foot. Alice gently pushed him aside. She leaned down and opened the letter slot and said, "Please open the door, Jimbo. If you don't, we'll call your dad."

There was a loud bump from within the house. Something clattered. Then footsteps padded toward them.

The door swung open.

Chief Jimbo, a handkerchief wadded under his nose,

stared at them with the forlorn expression of a kid who's sick and wants you to know it.

"I don't feel well," he said, his voice muffled by her handkerchief.

"You felt well enough to go to Tilbury Town," Mayor MacDonald said.

Chief Jimbo shook his head. "I should've stayed in bed."

"You should've kept Sheriff Cutter out of the investigation. That's what you should've done. And now you need to be at the Christmas fair. This is your jurisdiction, not Cutter's."

"Sheriff Cutter promised to keep me informed," Chief Jimbo said in a small voice.

"He did, did he?" Mayor MacDonald's face had gone crimson. "I bet he did…"

Alice stepped in, trying to be the voice of reason. "Chief Jimbo, don't you think you ought to be by Sheriff Cutter's side? Sooner or later, he's going to need to go back to Tilbury Town, and then who's going to be in charge?"

"It's taken care of," he mumbled. "My dad suggested if I ever needed help, I could call an old friend of his…"

"What do you mean?"

Chief Jimbo looked away. He looked ashamed.

"Jimbo?" She tried to catch his eye. "What did you do? Who did you call?"

CHAPTER 22

On the way back to the Christmas fair, Alice and Mayor MacDonald got stuck in traffic. Cars slowed to a crawl. The driver in front of them rolled down his window and leaned out, honking and shouting, "Move it, will you?"

But soon it became clear why traffic was so dense.

A state trooper directed traffic while his partner studied each passing car, occasionally stopping one to ask for ID. As Chief Jimbo had eventually confessed to them, he'd called the State Police's Bureau of Criminal Investigations, the head of which was an old golfing buddy of his dad's. Now the state police had descended on Blithedale, and there were cops everywhere, milling in and out of businesses and, which became clear as they crept closer, thronging the Christmas fair.

"I can't believe it," Mayor MacDonald muttered. "I can't believe he called the state police. This is bad…"

"How bad?"

Mayor MacDonald grimaced. "Disastrous. There's only

one person who dislikes Sheriff Cutter more than I do, and that's Captain Burlap, the Chief State Criminal Investigator."

Alice spotted Becca and Ona standing by the entrance to the fair.

"I'll get out here," Alice said and opened the passenger side door. She jumped out. The mayor's SUV drifted on down Main Street as Alice greeted Becca and Ona. Her friends at once began talking over each other.

Ona said, "The state police, they're everywhere and—"

"Where's Chief Jimbo?" Becca cut in.

"—they're taking over the investigation."

"They shut down the stage and the entire staff-only area, and now people are leaving."

Becca gestured toward the fair. As the sheriff's officers and state troopers flowed into the fair, civilians flowed out, parents tugging their kids along. Alice groaned. This was a disaster, exactly what they'd all worried would happen.

Sheriff Cutter stood in the crowd, barking commands at both his officers and state troopers. Somehow, he'd taken charge. Alice wondered how it worked. Blithedale was Chief Jimbo's jurisdiction. But it was part of Tilbury County, which was the sheriff's jurisdiction, which was part of the state, of course. How did they all get along?

Even as she wondered about that, she got her answer. A man in a state police uniform blocked Sheriff Cutter from entering the fair. Alice guessed this was Captain Burlap.

The sheriff's walrus mustache hung low in a deep frown while the captain gesticulated, making decisive movements with his hands. Cutter shook his head. Burlap pointed at him. It looked like he was giving Cutter a warning. Sheriff Cutter spun around and stomped away.

Captain Burlap called after him. "This is our investigation, Cutter. Stay out of our way!"

Cutter didn't turn around as he trudged away.

"Jeez," Ona said. "The boys don't know how to share, do they?"

"This is bad," Alice said, realizing that she was repeating what the mayor had said.

As they watched, the sheriff gathered his crew of officers and headed into the fair. Captain Burlap waved at nearby troopers and, together, they pursued the sheriff, pressing past the fairground guests who were milling out, many of them looking harried and harassed.

A little boy asked his dad, "What's going on, daddy?"

"Something bad," the dad said. "Must be with so many cops. Let's get out of here."

A familiar face emerged from the crowd and hurried down the sidewalk.

"Mariella Ridgeway," Alice said. "Let's see where she's going."

Becca said, "Sorry, I'm needed at the diner."

"We'll fill you in later," Ona said, and Alice grabbed her hand and tugged her down the street, following Mariella.

Mariella moved away from the fair. Alice worried she was headed to a car and that they wouldn't reach her in time. Once again, she'd slip away, leaving their questions unanswered.

But Mariella passed businesses and their parking lots—many of them closed, their owners manning stalls at the fair—until she came to the public library. She pulled open the door and stepped inside. A moment later, Alice and Ona followed her.

And walked right into Mariella.

"Oh, sorry," Alice said.

Mariella was standing just inside the door. Beyond her, Alice caught sight of Lorraine Maxwell, the librarian, peering over the circulation desk and giving her a friendly wave. Then she vanished from view again.

Mariella frowned. "Excuse me."

She made to move around Alice, stepping to the right. But Alice stepped to the right, too, and for a moment, they did a little doorway dance. Finally, they stopped and looked at each other.

"Actually," Alice said. "I was hoping to talk to you."

Mariella shook her head. "I've got a packed schedule, and I'm already late." She checked her wristwatch. "If I had my car, I'd already be at our offices, but Ben's borrowing it. Visiting his girlfriend. So here I am, waiting for a cab."

She let out a sigh and looked through the glass pane in the door, checking the public library's parking lot.

"No cab yet," Alice said. "So, why don't we take a couple of minutes to talk?"

"Fine. But when the cab gets here, I have to hustle."

"We need to know some things about Wade."

Mariella made a face. "I already told Chief Jimbo everything. And Sheriff Cutter. And a guy from the State Bureau of Criminal Investigations."

"Please," Alice said.

Again, Mariella looked at her watch and then out at the parking lot. "All right. What do you need to know?"

"You and your husband..." Alice said. "Were you close?"

"Let's cut the preamble. Did we have a good marriage? No. He was a liar, and he tried to steal from my business and from my clients. Was I going to divorce him? You better believe it. Another week and I would've served him the papers."

"How do you think he would've reacted?"

"He would've fought me." She shrugged. "But I would've won. I got the best lawyers. And I've got the law on my side. Besides documented cases of theft, he was cheating on me."

Alice and Ona exchanged glances. Alice said, "You caught him cheating?"

"I saw him sitting in a parked car with her. And when I asked him about it, he denied it. But I checked his phone one time and saw he made several calls to her. That's enough for me."

"Who was it?"

"Abigail Digby." She said the name with distaste. "That phony. But then Wade was a phony, too." Her face screwed up with distaste. "I only wish Ben wasn't mixed up with that family. He's a good kid, my son, and he can do better than a Digby."

"He knows Abigail Digby?"

"Of course he knows her, but it's the daughter, Kendra, he hangs out with. How he stomachs all her new-age silliness, I don't know. But at least she's not a 'socialite'—" She made air quotes with her fingers. "—like her mom."

"And what about her dad?"

Alice thought of Clyde Digby, the quiet, soft-spoken romance author, and wondered what he thought of his own wife.

"He keeps to himself," Mariella said. "And who can blame him?"

Mariella had confirmed what Mohammad told them about Wade's unethical behavior, and the picture of an unhappy marriage was clear. But what about the leather pouch?

"Do you know Vickers?"

Mariella smiled. "The cops asked about him, too. The answer is yes, I know Vickers. He arranges the Santa contest, of course, but a couple of years ago, Ridgeway Cleaning also relied on Vickers & Vickers' Plant Nursery to supply office plants. But I ended the contract. Vickers simply wasn't reliable—he'd cut corners, even tried to fiddle with the invoices to get more money than we owed him."

"And did the cops show you the leather pouch that Wade was carrying?"

"They showed me a documents case, yes."

She perked up, craning her neck to look past Alice.

Alice turned and saw a taxi pulling into the public library's parking lot.

"Excuse me," Mariella said, reaching for the door.

"And?" Alice said. "The pouch?"

Mariella pushed open the door, letting the cold air stream into the library lobby. "Same style. Same brand. But Wade's had a brass snap, and this one was silver." She smiled. "Sorry, but that wasn't my husband's case."

The door swung shut. Alice and Ona watched Mariella stride toward the taxi.

"So," Ona said with a sigh, "the leather pouch is a dead end."

"Maybe. But it tells us something important."

"What? That Vickers isn't the killer?"

"Yes, and that it's not what the killer wanted us to believe."

Ona gave her a sharp look. "Of course. The pouch was planted—pardon the pun—in Vickers' nursery, wasn't it?"

Alice nodded. Then added, "But why? Why frame Vickers?"

As they considered that question, Lorraine cleared her throat. Alice and Ona turned toward the circulation desk. Lorraine was resting her arms on the countertop and leaning toward them.

"Did you hear about the fair and the murder investigation? I just got a call from a friend..."

Alice nodded, approaching the desk along with Ona.

"Yeah, it's a mess. Ever since Sheriff Cutter took charge..."

Lorraine shook her head. "Not Cutter, no. A guy named Captain Burlap's in charge."

"Either way, the cops will drive the customers away."

"Not just drive them away, Alice. Captain Burlap shut down the fair."

"He what?!" Alice and Ona said in unison.

"Effective immediately," Lorraine said. "The whole fair is considered a crime scene."

CHAPTER 23

That night, Alice, Becca, and Ona gathered in the kitchen of the Pemberley Inn to make mulled wine. They'd talked about making an alcohol-free batch. But after the day's disastrous turn of events, Ona had insisted on regular wine, plus a splash of brandy.

"We need something to warm us," she said. "I feel chilled to the bone."

"And it's not just the drafty windows," Alice said, slicing an orange.

The gathering, which should've been cozy, felt gloomy. The awful news had hit them all hard. Without Christmas fair visitors, Main Street was desolate. Ona had done the best she could for the out-of-towners at the inn who'd traveled to Blithedale hoping to enjoy the fair. Alice expected tomorrow's business at Wonderland Books to be a disappointment.

Becca, who was adding cinnamon and cloves to the pot of simmering wine, sighed. "I still can't believe the state police closed down the Christmas fair. After all the hard work that everyone's done. And they're not saying when they'll allow it to open again, are they?"

Ona shook her head. "Nope. Honestly, this all boils down to a bunch of men fighting over territory."

"Well, to be fair, someone did commit a murder," Becca said. "Maybe all these law enforcement teams will solve the case, and we'll get our Christmas fair back in time for Christmas."

"Maybe," Alice said doubtfully.

A silence fell over them. They stood at the kitchen counter, preparing the mulled wine. Behind them was a couch—and next to that, the door to the pantry.

Alice got another fresh orange from the pantry.

Back at the counter, she grated the orange to provide zest for the mulled wine. Meanwhile, she gazed out the window at the inn's long backyard.

A blanket of snow covered Ona's tiny houses, which she built in her spare time. She built them quicker than she could sell them. There were so many of them, they made a village.

"What will happen if the fair doesn't reopen in time for Christmas?" Ona asked.

"It will have to," Becca said. "You know that."

"I know Mayor MacDonald took out a short-term loan to fund the fair. We all know that. But what happens if Blithedale can't pay it back in time?"

"The town may face legal action. The budget for next year will be drained. Services will be reduced or even canceled completely. The public library. The police department. Road maintenance. Garbage trucks. Other public utilities, like water and street lights. Everything restricted or shut down."

That put a damper on the conversation. Nobody said anything for a long while.

Then Becca said, "Can we move it to a new location? We could dismantle the stalls and then rebuild them somewhere else."

Ona shook her head. "Even if they'd allow us to haul off

the stalls, they wouldn't let us into the crime scene to do the work."

"You're right. It was a silly idea."

Ona touched Becca's arm. "Nothing silly about your ideas. How about some music to cheer us up?"

She paired her phone with a speaker in the kitchen and put on a playlist of holiday tunes. Alice appreciated the attempt at cheering everyone up. But the familiar, jolly songs only reminded her of the Christmas fair and the disaster the whole town would face if it remained closed over the holidays.

"Here," Ona said, stirring the pot with mulled wine. "Try some."

She scooped a cup into the dark-red, almost black, liquid, wiped the sides with a paper towel, and handed it to Alice. Then did the same for Becca. Finally, she served herself.

"To happy holidays," she said.

"And a white Christmas," Becca added.

Alice raised her cup. "And lots of presents."

Ona's eyes widened. "Oh, that reminds me."

She put down her cup and hurried over to the couch. A book lay on the seat, and Ona picked it up. Alice and Becca gathered around her.

"You gotta read this."

Alice grabbed the book and studied the cover.

What I Did For a Duke was the title. A woman was reaching up to kiss a man. Hair flowing off both their heads. Eyes closed in anticipation. Flowing white robes…

"A romance novel?" Alice asked.

"You say it as if that's a shameful thing." Ona put a hand on a hip and cocked her head, staring at Alice. "Alice, don't tell me you've got a bias against romance novels?"

"Well…"

"Then you really have to read this." Ona grinned. "And

then tell me if it doesn't keep you up all night—and keep you nice and warm."

Alice laughed. "Now that does sound appealing."

She turned the book over.

"The blurb says this is the fifth book in the series."

Then she saw the name of the series. She gaped.

It was book 5 in the Pennyroyal Green Series by Julie Anne Long.

She said, "Ona, did someone give this to you as a present?"

"How did you guess?"

"And was it an anonymous gift—a secret Santa?"

"Hold on." Ona gave her a little shove. "It was you, wasn't it? I thought maybe it was."

Alice shook her head. "No, it wasn't me. But I have the first four books in the series at Wonderland. Someone left them in my donation box."

"Wow, what a coincidence."

Alice stared at Ona, one eyebrow raised.

"Oh," Ona said.

"What?" Becca asked. "What am I missing?"

Alice shared her theory: A secret Santa was gifting books anonymously to people in Blithedale, matching them with books they would love—and then ensuring the rest of the books in that series were available at Wonderland Books.

"What amazes me," Alice said, "is that the person has identified books that a person would love so much. Even if that person didn't expect to."

She told them about Todd Townsend, and how surprised he'd been to discover that he loved Elena Ferrante's writing. That led them to speculate about who the secret Santa might be. It would have to be someone who loved books and knew people in town.

"Lorraine Maxwell," Becca said. "Who but a librarian could pull off something like this?"

Alice thought about it. "True. But she got a gift herself."

"Maybe she pretended to get a gift to throw us sleuths off the scent." Becca smiled. "Whoever's doing it has a strong sense of the holiday spirit. I wonder if it's someone involved with the Christmas fair…"

The mention of the Christmas fair sucked the joy out of them all, and the old, unhappy silence came back. Ona put aside her book.

"Let's have some more mulled wine," Alice suggested, eager to end the funk.

She crossed the floor to the kitchen counter and refilled their cups.

Looking out the window, she saw that it was snowing again. Big flakes were drifting down, adding to the blanket on the tiny house village. The miniature houses looked like what she imagined elves might live in. It was like the inn had its own Christmas Town in the backyard.

Which gave her an idea. "Ona, I bet we could run electricity to the tiny houses." She pointed out the window. "And then put up some porta-potties over there…"

Ona stepped over to the counter. A smile spread across her face. "Oh, my…"

Becca joined them, saying, "Wait, what are you talking about?"

Alice raised a cup of mulled wine, as if making a toast. "There's no need to reclaim our stalls, ladies. Let the cops have the fair. We've got a Christmas village right here in our backyard."

CHAPTER 24

*E*arly the next morning—before the breakfast rush—
Alice, Becca, and Ona sat in a booth at the diner.
They huddled around Alice's phone, which was on speaker
so everyone could hear. First, they called Mayor MacDonald,
who immediately loved the plan. He promised to contact
Abigail Digby and Mariella Ridgeway about moving to a new
location.

"I'll talk to Mariella about logistics," he said. "She'll move
fast—she always does."

After hanging up, Alice and her friends ate breakfast.
They talked about the tiny house village, and how they could
ensure it would become an even more magical experience
than the original Christmas fair.

Then the mayor called back: the plan got the green light.

"And we've got everything we need," he said.

Mariella Ridgeway's staff would bring in the trans-
formers and electrical cables later today, he explained. They
would also deliver porta-potties and set up a stage.

"And she's got a lead on a giant Christmas tree, plus decorations."

He promised to call them later to confirm the delivery time.

After he hung up, Ona said, "Now we need to let the vendors know."

"We'll have to give them clear instructions," Alice said.

"That's right," Becca said. "They need to know which tiny house they can occupy."

"Already taken care of."

Ona unfolded a large piece of paper and spread it out on the table, pushing plates and cups aside. Alice and Becca leaned over the table.

"This is amazing," Becca said.

Ona had drawn a detailed map of the Pemberley Inn's backyard, detailing every tiny house. The map included porta-potties and a small stage, plus lines showing where they'd run electrical cables.

"I love a reliable map," Ona said, grinning. "Almost as much as I love a process."

She placed another sheet of paper over the map. At the top of the paper, she'd listed a bullet-pointed process, explaining to vendors how to access the new fairgrounds and set up their shops. Below that was a list of vendors with phone numbers. She'd marked each vendor with an A, B, or O.

Ona explained: "You can use the bullet-point process as a script. The vendors marked with an 'A' are yours, Alice. Becca, you call these vendors marked 'B.' I'll take the rest."

She'd made copies of both the map and the list of vendors for them.

Alice, taking her copy of the papers, said, "Ona, you really are a superhero."

"You're one of a kind," Becca agreed.

The three of them spent the next hour calling vendors. They reached most of them. The few vendors Alice hadn't talked to, she marked on her sheet. She would try calling them after she opened Wonderland Books for the day.

By then, the diner was buzzing with activity, and Becca got to work. Alice finished her coffee, eager to get to her bookstore and check the donations box. Did the secret Santa drop off more books?

Ona said, "I'd better go back to the inn, in case Mariella shows up with her staff."

They wrestled back into their coats and scarves and headed out into the winter weather. The sky was an icy blue. The air was so cold it burned, and when Alice drew in a deep breath, the cold flowed into her chest with a freshness that reminded her of strong mints.

Ona waved a goodbye and headed up the front porch steps to the inn, while Alice continued down the street. Her tiny-house log cabin, festooned with heavy snow, looked especially festive today. But at the path that led to the front door, she hesitated. Further down the street, past the consignment store, stood Kendra Digby's new age shop.

A couple of minutes later, Alice was knocking on the front door. The sign above her head said, "Mystic Tree Readings & Remedies," and there was that tree-of-life logo again. Faintly, through the walls, she could hear the drone of sitar music. She knocked again.

Finally, the lock snicked, and the door opened. Kendra stuck her head out.

"I don't open for another fifteen minutes."

"I'd like to talk to you about the Christmas fair."

"Oh, sure."

Kendra opened the door wide and stepped back, hugging herself against the cold. Alice closed the door behind her. It was almost oppressively hot in the little shop, and she unzipped her coat.

The smell of incense was strong. The entire back wall,

next to a small counter, comprised pigeon holes with small jars of tea. Crystals, new age trinkets, and books by healers and clairvoyants cluttered the display tables. Beyond the counter, through an open door, Alice glimpsed a back room with a long work table—large jars of loose teas and herbs suggested this was where Kendra mixed her infusions.

In the middle of the floor, Kendra had rolled out a yoga mat.

"Sorry, did I interrupt your yoga?" Alice said.

"My morning meditation. But it's fine. It's my own fault." She laughed. She had a bright laugh, like the chatter of a tropical bird. "After all, I called you here."

"You called me?" Alice instinctively put a hand in her pocket to check her phone for a missed call. "I didn't realize—"

"I've been worried about the fair being shut down and all the business I'm losing out on. But during my meditation—" Kendra crouched down and rolled up the yoga mat. "—I centered my thoughts on the Christmas fair to allow the universe to guide me toward a solution. And here you are."

"Right. Here I am." Alice gestured at the display tables and the shelves with teas. "What a pretty store. You must do well for yourself."

"My dad helps out," Kendra said with unexpected frankness.

Kendra must've noticed Alice's surprise, because she added, "I balance the books myself. My profits are my own doing. But if it weren't for dad, I could never have opened this store. How would I have gotten the start-up capital?"

Alice thought of her friends, Becca and Ona, and how they'd established the Blithedale Future Fund to invest in her bookstore. Without their help, there would be no Wonderland Books. She didn't judge Kendra for getting help from her rich dad.

"Soon, I'll be more independent, though," Kendra said. "I'll start paying Dad back. And I'll be moving out. I'm going to find a place of my own. I have no desire to be like my mom—always living off my dad's money." She struggled with some emotion—irritation, concern, anger?—and then suppressed it. She smiled again. "So, tell me, what's the plan for the Christmas fair?"

Alice explained the fair would move from its present location to the Pemberley Inn's backyard, with each vendor occupying a tiny house.

Kendra nodded, a half smile on her face, as if she was patiently letting Alice tell her something she already knew.

"So those are the details," Alice finished. "By tomorrow morning, you can find your tiny house and get set up."

"When the planets align, fate moves fast."

And when Ona gets organized, Alice thought, *things move even faster.*

"We're lucky the Ridgeway Cleaning staff can set things up today," Alice said.

"More work for poor Ben."

Alice wondered about that comment. The way Kendra said it, with a hint of genuine concern, it seemed overwork might be a real problem for Ben.

"It must be a lot," Alice said. "The cleaning business and now also the Christmas fair. Does he feel a lot of stress?"

"I wouldn't call it stress." Kendra sighed. She dropped her voice, as if she were afraid someone would overhear. Though they were, of course, alone. She said, "Ben suffers from anxiety. He didn't grow up in a happy home, you know. He's told me things that would break your heart."

"The two of you are—?" Alice left her sentence unfinished, raising an eyebrow.

Kendra made a dismissive gesture. "Oh, just good friends."

But she looked away, as if she wasn't being completely honest.

Maybe they are "just" good friends, but she wants more?

"You hang out a lot together," Alice said.

"He comes to my house a lot, yeah. It's like a second home for him—you know, a place he can crash and feel at home. A safe space. My store is a safe space, too. He comes here to relax and drink my serenity tea—he says it's the only thing that helps his anxiety. After what his dad did…"

"What did his dad do?"

"He stole money from the family."

Alice nodded.

Kendra said, "But there's more…"

She leaned close, and Alice got a hint of what Kendra would be like with her customers: intimate and gossipy. It was a combination that would attract many people, no doubt.

Kendra whispered, "Ben discovered his dad was black-mailing people."

"Really?" Alice feigned surprise. "Which people?"

"Someone Ben worked with."

"At Ridgeway Cleaning?"

"I don't think so." Kendra frowned. "Someone involved with the fair. He didn't say who. But I could tell, because he'd come from some meetings with the organizers and volunteers about the fair, and that's when he mentioned what his dad was doing. I made the connection."

Clearly, Kendra didn't know as much about this gossip as she would've liked. But she was proud of the connections she made on her own.

Blithedale is full of us amateur sleuths, Alice thought.

To be fair, if it was true, this was interesting information. Whoever Wade had been blackmailing had a motive to kill him. If Ben had identified the blackmailing victim, he might actually have identified the killer. And if the killer was part of the Christmas fair team, then Alice had a clear list of suspects.

Someone involved with the Christmas fair logistics, maybe—or the Santa contest.

One name jumped out at her.

"Ben didn't mention Vickers, did he?"

Something passed over Kendra's face, a flash of disgust. "No, but Vickers is the kind of man who would be involved in blackmail."

"I thought you said Wade was involved in blackmail."

"Two people can be blackmailers, can't they?" Kendra narrowed her eyes. "I know Vickers. I once worked at his plant nursery. He's a disgusting man. He made a pass at me after we closed the store. I never went back."

It didn't surprise Alice that Vickers would do something like that. But she didn't see the connection to blackmailing. Unless Wade had been blackmailing Vickers, of course.

Kendra must've sensed her doubt, because she leaned close and said, "Trust me. If anyone's done something bad, it's Vickers."

Someone knocked at the door, and Kendra walked away from Alice. She pulled open the door.

"Oh, hi—yes, I'm opening now."

As Kendra's first customer of the day stepped inside, Alice took it as her cue to leave, too. Wonderland Books also needed to open for the day.

She thanked Kendra for her help.

As she was leaving, she thought about what Kendra had said. Could she be right—was Vickers a killer? Or was it what Kendra wanted her to believe?

CHAPTER 25

*W*hile Alice helped customers find books, her conversation with Kendra Digby swirled in her mind. She emptied the donations box, finding only a handful of books this time, and most of them no good. And she restocked shelves. But she moved like a sleepwalker, her body going through the motions, as her mind strayed far from the bookstore.

As she grabbed a box of books and hauled it over to the shelves for restocking, she pictured Wade's body in the trailer, the deadly cup of hot chocolate in front of him. She thought of Vickers' nursery and the hidden leather document case. And she considered everything she'd learned about the Ridgeways and the Digbys.

She was considering the facts—and a few guesses—when Sheriff Cutter entered the bookstore. He lumbered inside, dragging snow with him.

"Sheriff," she said. "Are you looking for a book?"

"Book." He snorted. "I'm paying you a courtesy visit."

"Lucky me."

He gave her a sharp look, obviously catching her snarky

tone. She couldn't help it. She didn't like the man. He exuded an I-know-best, it's-my-way-or-the-highway attitude that she found repulsive. But then he didn't seem to like her, either.

With his hands gripping his belt buckle, he stared daggers at her.

"I know you and Chief Jimbo are cozy. But this is my investigation now—"

"I thought the state police were in charge," she said innocently.

His face flushed. "Leave that to me. In any case, you'll stay out of it."

He stared at her, clearly expecting a response. She realized that he'd come to her bookstore to impress on her that he was in charge. A man who was in charge wouldn't have the time—or the need—to do that.

She didn't reply to his demand.

He can bully me all he wants. He won't extract a promise from me to stay away.

Finally, he said, "Well, that's all."

"Thanks." She smiled and indicated the door. "Have a nice day."

On his way out, he glanced over his shoulder, scowling at her. She watched him walk down the path to his cruiser, which stood parked by the curb. He got in, slammed the door, and drove off.

That clinched it for her. Even though the sheriff and the state police were investigating Wade's death, she wouldn't withdraw. She'd come this far. She wanted to know who murdered Wade.

And maybe she also wanted to annoy Sheriff Cutter.

So what loose ends should she pick up?

Mariella Ridgeway had revealed that the leather pouch found at Vickers & Vickers wasn't Wade's. And that she was divorcing her husband. What secrets might Abigail Digby harbor?

I'll need to talk to her, Alice thought as she slipped books into empty spaces on the shelves. *But with two outside law enforcement agencies involved, I'd better be careful. They won't appreciate an amateur detective snooping around.*

She was shelving a book by Elena Ferrante, *The Days of Abandonment,* which made her think of Todd Townsend and his recent infatuation with Ferrante's books.

Nobody would question Todd's right to ask questions. That was the benefit of being a journalist. *The Blithedale Record* had run stories on the Christmas fair, but none of them had focused on Abigail Digby. So Todd even had an excuse...

It might just work.

She dug into her pocket, fumbling for her phone. Then found the contact and made the call.

"Alice," Todd said on the other end. "You got another murder story for me?"

"No, but I have an interview."

"Oh?"

"With Abigail Digby."

He laughed. "Did she put you up to this? That snob's been practically demanding an interview for months."

"That's great news."

Todd went silent. She could almost hear him thinking across the line. Then he said, sounding wary, "Alice, what are you up to this time?"

CHAPTER 26

The Digbys mansion lay nestled in the Blithedale Woods. But the half-mile-long drive was nothing like the usual dirt roads in the forest. It was smoothly paved, the trees and undergrowth cut back, leaving plenty of room for cars to pass each other.

The house itself was massive. Bigger than the Pemberley Inn. In fact, bigger than any other building she'd seen in Blithedale. It was a modern home comprising two large gable-roofed wings connected with a steel-and-glass cube in the middle.

As they drove toward it, Alice craned over the dashboard, gazing ahead.

"You think they have enough space in there?"

"Enough to divide the kingdom in half," Todd said.

She gave him a questioning look. He shrugged. "I hear Mr. Digby likes his privacy."

"Even from his wife?"

"Especially from his wife. According to the grapevine, Clyde and his daughter occupy the west wing and Abigail lives in the east wing. They're one big happy family—as long as they're not together."

The drive swung to the right and curved into a circular driveway. Todd pulled the car over to the side, parking. Next to his car stood two cruisers, a state police car and one from the Tilbury County Sheriff's Department.

Oh, terrific, Alice thought.

She got out on the passenger side and looked up at the house. A pathway led to stairs, which rose to the steel-and-glass cube and its front door.

Before they'd even reached the door, it opened.

Sheriff Cutter stood in the doorway. When he saw her, his frown turned to a glare. Alice didn't let him intimidate her.

"Miss Hartford," the sheriff said icily as they approached.

"I see you two have already met," Todd said, patting the sheriff on the shoulder.

He ignored Todd. To Alice, he said, "I told you to stay out of this."

Captain Burlap stepped out of the house, shouldering past Sheriff Cutter. Behind them stood a butler, a woman in a blue suit with a white shirt and white tie.

"Wow, did we miss a party?" Todd said. "All we're missing is the FBI."

"Funny you should mention the FBI." Captain Burlap shook Todd's hand. Then he turned to Sheriff Cutter and said, "Cutter, why don't you rustle up those reports I requested?"

Sheriff Cutter muttered a curse and headed down the steps.

Captain Burlap continued, "Wade Ridgeway was under investigation for cyber crimes. We're working with the FBI on that part. We believe he'd been targeting old folks on the internet, scamming them out of their retirement savings. But we didn't expect to get involved in a murder case until we got a call from your chief of police."

"And you came here to ask the Digbys some questions?"

"Routine stuff. It seems your chief of police didn't follow procedure on how to conduct official interviews and make statements. Call this a version 2.0."

Todd chuckled. "Chief Jimbo's work is usually a beta version."

Captain Burlap headed down toward his cruiser. Meanwhile, the butler welcomed Alice and Todd, offering to take their coats. Abigail Digby strode out of a doorway, her high heels clicking across the massive, marble-floored entrance hall.

"Darlings," she said, holding out her arms. "I'm delighted you could visit. Absolutely delighted. Come, come…"

Alice thanked the young woman who took her coat, feeling uncomfortable about the formality of it all. She followed Abigail and Todd through a corridor, up three steps, and then into a living room that could've doubled as a cathedral. She gazed up at the distant ceiling. The fireplace was half the size of Wonderland Books. There were two sets of couches and armchairs. Billboard-sized art on the walls. A life-sized Greek goddess sculpture that looked a lot like—

"Uh," Alice said, looking at the white marble statue. "Is that you, Mrs. Digby?"

"Call me Abigail, please. And come sit."

Todd lowered his lanky body into an armchair. Alice perched on the edge of a loveseat, momentarily distracted by a piece of red cloth that seemed to be caught underneath. Then Abigail draped herself across a sofa, which was covered with some kind of fur, and spoke.

"Something sweet?"

She pointed to a bowl of caramels on the glass coffee table that separated the three of them.

When no one accepted her offer, she said, "Darlings, to what do I owe the pleasure?" She leaned back, closed her eyes, affecting a saintly pose. "Ask me anything—I'm used to it by now."

Alice was about to do just that—she had lots of questions about the murder—but Todd held out a hand, cautioning her.

"Mind if I record this?" Todd asked.

"Why not?"

He placed his phone on the glass coffee table. Then said, "Abigail, tell us how you were selected to headline the Christmas fair."

Alice noticed the word choice: "selected" and "headline." She understood what he was doing—flattering her.

"Oh, that," she swatted at the air, dismissing it as nothing. "They naturally wanted someone with experience. Someone who understands how to inspire an audience. It was pure luck that I had a gap in my schedule."

For a while, Todd indulged her ego, ensuring he presented her in a favorable light. She talked about her involvement in charitable events in the city and how a life-style magazine had run a special feature about her. He got her to expand on the philosophy of Christmas, and how giving came easily to her—she was, she assured them, hopelessly generous.

Then he said, "Then the murder happened and the Christmas fair closed."

For an instant, she looked confused by the abrupt change of topic. Then it passed.

"Yes," she said simply.

"Did you know Wade Ridgeway?"

She sat up. She brushed the hair back from her face. "Not really."

"Not really?"

"His wife, Mariella—" She made a face. "—handles all the cleaning and such things for the fair. Since I'm the host of the entire show, it's been necessary for me to work with her. Her husband hung around the staff-only area."

Alice joined the conversation. "He was taking part in the Santa contest."

Abigail barked a laugh. "Don't be ridiculous. That man was the least likely Santa in the world. I hear his own wife barred him from entering the staff-only area, and so he enrolled in the Santa contest, so he could hang around and be a nuisance."

"So he was a fraud?"

Abigail reached for the bowl of caramels and cradled it in her lap. She studied it, as if making a tough choice. Then selected one and popped it in her mouth.

"He was a nasty man," she said to the bowl of caramels. "Everyone knows that."

"Yes, but you seem to know more about it than others," Alice said.

Abigail set down the bowl on the glass table with a loud clack.

"I'm really not interested in Wade Ridgeway," she said brightly, a rigid smile on her face. "How about we talk about the Christmas fair and all the wonderful things about it? Now that it's moved to a new location, we can put this horrible murder business behind us."

Todd complied, jumping in with a series of questions about how she'd written her own speeches and what she thought could be improved at next year's fair. As Alice listened with increasing boredom to Abigail talk about her own talents, she glanced down and noticed the red fabric again. It was sticking out from beneath the love seat.

She reached down and tugging, only revealed more of it.

So she tugged again, and it kept coming. It was long. Before she knew it, she was holding a red scarf in her hands.

Abigail had gone quiet. She was staring at Alice.

Then she smiled. "Oh, kids. Kendra had a friend over. He must've left it."

"Ben Ridgeway?"

"That's right," she said lightly. But her voice had taken on a flatness, like someone reading a script. "He's friends with my daughter." Then she slid off the sofa and got to her feet. "Well, this certainly has been a lovely conversation…"

It was clear she wanted them to leave. Alice stood. Todd retrieved his phone and thanked Abigail profusely. Before turning to go, Alice held out the scarf. "Do you want to hold on to this?"

Abigail reached out. Then snapped back her hand.

"You can ask our butler to return it to Mr. Ridgeway," she said stiffly. "I'm sure you can find your way out."

Alice and Todd walked down the corridor toward the entrance hall.

"That was interesting," Alice said.

"Exactly the word I would've chosen," Todd said. "The talk about Wade made her uncomfortable, didn't it?"

And the talk about Ben Ridgeway, too…

At the front door, they didn't have to wait for more than a few seconds before the butler turned up with their coats. She opened the front door for them. Outside, a delivery truck pulled up and a uniformed man strode up the steps with a package. Alice recognized the logo on the box—it was from an online bookstore.

The butler took the box. "Mr. Digby's been waiting for these books."

She said goodbye and carried the books into the house, the door closing behind her.

Alice glanced up at the other wing of the house—opposite to the one they'd entered with Abigail Digby—and saw a bearded man standing at an enormous window, hands behind his back, looking down at her.

It was Clyde Digby. He was smiling.

CHAPTER 27

hat evening, Alice met Ona at the Woodlander Bar. It was far too cold to sit outside, the temperature having dropped again. The tiny house was packed with people. But Alice had arrived early enough to secure two seats around a small table.

Thor, the bartender and owner, had made them mulled apple cider with bourbon. Lewis Tuttle, still helping Thor, served the drinks.

The mulled cider warmed Alice from the inside, and she felt herself thaw.

"It sounds like Abigail Digby is hiding something," Ona said after Alice filled her in. "Obviously, she hated Wade Ridgeway."

Alice nodded. "But lots of people did. It doesn't mean she killed him."

"What did you make of the scarf?"

Alice had thought a lot about Ben's scarf and Abigail's reaction.

"She seemed eager to get us out after I found the scarf. But why? Everyone knows Ben and Kendra spend a lot of time together. I get the sense that Kendra is trying to move the friendship toward something more romantic."

She told Ona about her visit to Kendra's shop.

Ona said, "Maybe Abigail Digby feels awkward about her daughter being involved with a Ridgeway, the way Mariella felt about her son being involved with Kendra. After all, she detested Wade, and from what you say, I don't see Abigail and Mariella getting along, either."

"Yeah, maybe."

But Alice wasn't so sure. There was a detail about that scarf—something important—that she was missing. The thought brought back the image of Clyde Digby standing at that window in the west wing of the mansion and looking down at her.

But what did seeing Clyde Digby have to do with the red scarf?

There was the promise of an idea at the back of her mind, but it was a wispy thing, still too insubstantial to make sense of.

She shook her head. "Somehow these two unhappy couples—the Ridgeways and the Digbys—are at the center of this. But the picture isn't complete, and besides, the whole thing is thrown off balance by those two jokers..."

"Bunce and Vickers?"

At that moment, Lewis Tuttle passed their table. He stopped.

"Bunce and Vickers," he said. "Those two are as thick as thieves."

"You know them?"

"Bunce won the Santa contest last year, and he used to run the bookstore in Blithedale, so of course I knew of him. He's not a friend. His only friend seems to be Vickers."

"They're actual friends?" Ona said, sounding surprised. "I didn't know Bunce had friends."

Lewis shrugged. "Good enough friends for Bunce to be staying at Vickers' house. I heard them talking about it. Apparently Bunce has made himself comfortable in the guest room."

Lewis hurried over to another table to clear the empty glasses and make his way back to the bar.

Alice felt foolish. She'd gotten Chief Jimbo and Sheriff Cutter involved in looking at Vickers' office, but they'd all failed to examine the man's home.

Ona leaned closer to Alice. "I say we drop by Vickers' home tomorrow. Take a look around. What do you say?"

"Good idea." Alice sipped her drink, considering Bunce and Vickers' role in the murder case. "Let's assume they stole that Santa bag from the trailer. Why? What's so important that it's worth breaking into a crime scene? And why did that leather pouch turn up at the plant nursery, obviously left there by the killer to implicate Vickers?"

"Maybe the killer wanted to distract attention from themselves and picked Vickers, because the killer doesn't like Vickers. Maybe Vickers did something to the killer."

Ona made a good point. The killer had ensured Wade—and only Wade—drank the poison, apparently not wanting other people to get hurt. Except framing Vickers was OK. So, what had Vickers done to the killer?

Alice sipped the last of her mulled apple cider, bracing for the burn of bourbon down her throat. But it was sweetened by maple syrup and softened by the spiced cider.

Lewis came to their table and cleared their empty glasses. He offered to get them another round from the bar, which Ona was quick to say yes to. He hurried off.

Alice was thinking, trying to remember. Someone had recently expressed their dislike of Vickers.

She said, "Mariella Ridgeway used to work with Vickers. Remember? He wasn't reliable, so she ended the contract."

"That's hardly a reason to frame someone."

"True." Then Alice had it. It wasn't Mariella who'd expressed the strongest dislike. It was Kendra. "Kendra Digby used to work for Vickers, but his behavior became inappropriate."

"Sexual harassment in the workplace?" Ona looked thoughtful. "That might give Kendra enough of a desire to frame Vickers. But what makes Kendra a likely killer?"

Alice shook her head, unable to come up with a believable answer. Wade had been engaged in blackmail. Why would he blackmail Kendra? Her dad might be rich, but otherwise, she wasn't rich—she was a young woman selling new-age books, crystals, and medicinal stuff. Spices and herbs. Not exactly a big moneymaker.

As she considered the question, she and Ona gazed over at the bar. Thor was drizzling ground spices into a cocktail shaker. He stirred the contents. Sniffed it. Then sprinkled more spices in before sealing and shaking it.

Spices, Alice thought, the word lighting up in her mind. *Spices and herbs...*

"Kendra sells a lot of medicinal teas," she mumbled, more to herself than to Ona. "I wonder what's in some of those teas."

Ona brought out her phone, the screen shining brightly in the dim lighting of the bar. "Easy to check that. Kendra's website lists the teas and their ingredients."

Alice leaned close to Ona, looking at the screen as Ona scrolled through lists of teas. There was the cold-and-flu tea that Chief Jimbo was drinking. And there was one for "flushing the kidneys and restoring spiritual balance." Another supported the immune system, also promising a "holistic strengthening and centering of your inner self."

Ona chuckled. "Judging by the descriptions, I could

become a superhuman if I drank all these teas. At least in large quantities."

The ingredients included nettles, echinacea, valerian, dandelion root, and dozens of plants that Alice had never thought to put in a tea—some of them she'd never even heard of before.

But one ingredient stood out.

"This stress-reliever," Alice said. "It contains aconite."

"Why do I know that name?"

"Because it's what killed Wade."

CHAPTER 28

he next morning, Alice and Ona passed Kendra's shop, but it was closed, and no one answered when they knocked. It was still early, they decided. And then there was the plan from the night before: They would visit Vickers' home, hoping to find clues to what Bunce and Vickers were up to.

Forty-five minutes later, Ona parked her pickup truck down the street from Vickers & Vickers' Plant Nursery. They didn't want to alert Bunce or Vickers to their approach, so they left the pickup and crept up to the entrance on foot.

The parking lot was as empty as before. Glancing through the open door to the store, Alice saw the teenager at the counter. He sat hunched over his phone, his fingers dug into his hair as he watched the screen, light flickering across his face. Behind him, the door to the office stood open. She waited. Was Vickers inside?

Then she heard him call out, "Coffee!"

The teenager looked up, an aggrieved frown on his face. But he tapped his phone and pushed away from the counter, launching his rolling desk chair toward a coffee machine.

She'd seen enough. She pulled away from the doorway.

"Vickers is inside," she whispered.

Ona nodded and stuck out a thumb, gesturing toward the back of the building. She went first, Alice following in her footsteps. Whenever they came to a window, they both crouched down and hurried past it, careful not to be seen.

At the end of the building, the property opened up. In spring, and in better times, this might have been a parkland of nursery plants, a delight for green-fingered shoppers. But now it was snow-covered, and Alice suspected, barren below.

Glancing back, Alice made sure that Vickers couldn't see them out of his office window. The blinds were down. Good. So she and Ona strode across the field, the crunch of snow sounding unnaturally loud, each step making her wince inwardly.

Up ahead, the house stood at the top of an incline where the property ended. Alice felt exposed. If Bunce was at the house and he looked out a window, he'd spot them trudging through the snow. But from a distance, they saw no movement.

They stepped up to the first window they got to and peered through the glass. A study. Rows of bookshelves. A mahogany desk. A sofa. Even through the grimy windows, the study looked dusty, long in disuse. Alice guessed this had once belonged to Vickers' father, the founder of Vickers & Vickers' Plant Nursery. Apparently, Vickers wasn't a reader, nor a man who enjoyed sitting at a hardwood desk and doing business.

She was beginning to see what Vickers and Bunce had in common.

Around the back, she and Ona came to a bank of large windows, and the interior of the house revealed what must be Vickers' favorite space: the living room. There was a massive flatscreen TV, a video game console and two controllers, empty pizza and fried-chicken takeout boxes, and superhero comic books scattered across the floor.

"Vickers is a bona fide man-boy," Ona muttered. "But where's—?"

Bunce walked into the room, carrying a bowl of popcorn and a six-pack of soda. He headed for the couch, plopped down, and pressed the remote control. The TV sprang to life.

"Too bad he's hone," Ona whispered. "How're we going to snoop around now?"

Alice tugged at Ona's sleeve. They moved away from the window.

Turning a corner, they came to a set of back steps. Obviously the kitchen. Beyond this must be the front door—Alice could see a snow-covered yard and a street in the distance.

Alice cupped her hands around her eyes and peered through a window into the kitchen. There was the edge of a kitchen counter. A table and chairs.

"Maybe the door's open," she whispered.

"You want to go inside?" Ona asked. "While Bunce is in there?"

"It's our best chance to find some clue to what they've been doing."

"You're nuts," Ona said, and broke into a grin. "And I love you for it."

Alice tried the kitchen door. It was unlocked. She eased it open, and it groaned. It sent prickles down her spine, and she froze. Distantly, she could hear the TV. She waited. When no sound of Bunce clomping toward them came, she pushed the door open.

The kitchen—linoleum floor, cheap compression-board cabinets, formica countertop—was a mess. The sink overflowed with dirty plates and glasses, and trash covered the counter, from pizza boxes to balled-up paper towels.

But it was notable for one other thing: In a corner stood a

box, and inside the box were more boxes. Lots of little boxes containing counterfeit smartphones.

Ona shook her head. "He didn't move them far, did he? If Sheriff Cutter had bothered to search Vickers' home…"

In the living room, Bunce shouted at the TV: "You fools!"

Alice and Ona exchanged glances.

Ona whispered, "Now what?"

Alice noticed a bit of burlap sticking up from behind the box of counterfeit smartphones. Coming around the side, she spotted the Ridgeway Cleaning logo on the side.

She crouched down, pulled the bag open, and, for once in her life hoping she wouldn't see Christmas presents, was gratified to see that it was full of slips of paper.

"Bingo."

Ona, looking over Alice's shoulder, said, "Not exactly what you expect Santa to deliver at Christmas, is it?"

"Unless you're Bunce, and all you want for Christmas is to win the Santa contest."

Alice dug into the sack and pulled out a handful of slips. They were identical. Each one was an official voting slip for the Santa contest. But they weren't blank. They had already been filled out, each one noting "Bunce" as the "Best Santa in Blithedale."

Ona gasped. Then put a hand over her mouth to stifle herself.

Alice said, "What do you say we call the cops?"

CHAPTER 29

*A*lice and Ona, retelling the story of how Bunce and Vickers had reacted when the Tilbury Town police department and state troopers descended on them, laughed again. They were strolling around the tiny house village behind the inn, checking on the progress the vendors had made in setting up and going back over what had happened.

Ona said, "And when we heard the sirens and Vickers came bolting out of the plant nursery building, seeing the patrol cars pulling up in front of his home...my God, I would never have guessed he could run so fast."

"Bunce's reaction was the funniest, though," Alice said. "Remember what he told the cops? 'Do you have any idea how expensive it is to retire to Florida!?'"

Ona laughed and shook her head. "It all makes sense now. They rigged the contest last year and split the proceeds. They were going to try again. That's why Bunce came to Blithedale for Christmas. That's why he was staying at Vickers' place."

"Well, that and because he's tight-fisted."

"So you think they went into the trailer to get the bag of slips—and only that?"

"I do," Alice said. "Those were the official, watermarked slips. They couldn't simply duplicate them. They needed to fill them out, making it look as if people had voted for Bunce. But then the murder happened. As long as the bag with slips was locked inside the trailer, Vickers and Bunce couldn't complete their plan."

"They had nothing to do with the murder."

"Nothing."

They continued to inspect the tiny houses. Occasionally, Ona would ask a vendor a question about their setup or check that they had what they needed. But it seemed the Ridgeway Cleaning staff had everything under control. The only thing missing was the Christmas tree—the vendor was late in delivering the tree.

Ona said, "I hope it comes tomorrow. Otherwise, we'll have to open the fair without a Christmas tree, and that's not good."

In the distance, Alice spotted Mohammad by the floats. He was on a ladder again, trying to reattach the reindeer's head.

"Poor Mohammad," Ona said. "The guy gets an A for effort. He's had to fix Rudolph several times already. He says the original stitching, which was very strong, broke, and now the repairs keep coming undone."

Alice also caught sight of Mariella striding through the tiny house village, stopping to talk to one of her employees before moving on to the next thing.

That woman never stops moving, Alice thought, and decided she admired Mariella's dedication to her business. Which reminded her of her own. She checked the time. Soon, she'd have to open Wonderland Books.

"I'll head over early to the bookstore," she told Ona. "See you later."

"Coffee first?" Ona suggested.

Bonsai & Pie, which had been allocated a Nantucket-style tiny house, was up and running, and Andrea made them each a complimentary coffee. After handing them their paper cups, she leaned out of the doorway, her big earrings jangling as she stared up at the sky.

"What do you think—another storm on the way?"

The wind was picking up again and dark clouds had rolled in.

"Weather forecaster's sitting on the fence," Andrea said. "Fifty-fifty chance."

"Those are better odds than at a casino," Ona said, glancing up at the sky. "Though the clouds do look pretty ominous."

Alice left them to their weather forecasting and, sipping her coffee, headed over to a gate in the fence. The gate led to a parking area for the inn's guests. She emerged from there onto Main Street and walked down the sidewalk.

Getting ready to cross the street, she glanced across at Wonderland Books. There was someone in front of the store. And that someone was bending over the donation box.

She stepped behind a tree, doing the best to hide.

The man—she was sure it was a man—tore open a box and pulled out books, dropping them into the donations box. Then he turned and strode down the path, the empty box in one hand.

It was Clyde Digby.

He glanced this way and that, then dropped the box into a public trash can before strolling down the sidewalk.

Once he was out of sight, Alice hurried over to the trash can. Digging out the box, she recognized it. It was identical to the one a delivery truck had brought to the Digby mansion while she and Todd visited Abigail. Maybe it was the same one.

She left it in the trash and hurried to her donation box.

She opened it. Inside were several used books—all the first books in well-known trilogies by Ken Follett, Amitav Ghosh, and V.E. Schwab. Alice turned and glanced back in the direction Clyde had gone.

She smiled to herself.

So Clyde Digby was the secret Santa.

Here was a bestselling author who'd lived in Blithedale for years. He bought sequels for people, leaving them anonymously, and then made sure that Alice had the corresponding first books in the series. And if she didn't, he'd provide them by ordering them online and donating them to her.

Why did he do it? She supposed the result spoke for itself. His little game had gotten people excited about reading—many of them buying more books at Wonderland. He must love books and bookstores as much as Alice did.

She was smiling as she unlocked her bookstore and stepped inside. She looked around at her log-cabin tiny house and the rows of books. It warmed her that someone else loved her bookstore enough to want to support it, and in such a creative way, too.

She left the books on the counter and pulled off her coat. Then took a sip of coffee and, turning around, jumped.

Lewis Tuttle was standing in front of her.

"You gave me a scare," she said.

"Sorry, Alice. I didn't mean to sneak up on you." He looked embarrassed, and it didn't pass. In halting words, he said, "See, I—well, the thing is...I wanted to ask if you're looking to hire anyone."

Thor couldn't keep him on, Lewis explained, and he'd been to most of the businesses in town, asking if they needed someone.

"Even if I win the Santa contest," he said, "I need something long term. For now, I've offered to volunteer at the

Christmas fair. Maybe if some of the people working there see that I can be useful…" He sighed. "But I need paid work."

Alice bit her lip. "I'm really sorry, Lewis. I know finding work in Blithedale is difficult, and I wish I could offer you something. But my business is small. I can't justify hiring another person, even part time. I'll ask around, though."

"Thanks, I really appreciate it."

He gave her a brave smile and left the bookstore.

The joy she'd felt at discovering Clyde Digby's secret had vanished. She could only think of poor Lewis Tuttle, who'd lost his business and now struggled to find decent work.

She turned her attention to the books on the counter, and she was halfway through the stack when a loud thud shook the tiny house.

What was that?

Another thud shook the house. It was as if someone or something was ramming it. She put down the books, struggled into her coat, and hurried outside.

Outside the bookstore, she couldn't see any sign of a problem. So she walked around the tiny house. Behind the bookstore, she noticed that something had dislodged the snow from the roof. Looking closer, she thought she saw the imprint of something that had pressed up against the wall. Below it, the snow was in disarray, but she could make out a footprint.

Like someone threw themselves against the wall, she thought. *But that's insane. Why would someone do that?*

She looked around. There were buildings on either side of Wonderland Books, but behind the bookstore—as behind every business on Main Street—the trees of the Blithedale Woods reared up. Since the trees were leafless, she could see far into the woods, and there was no sign of anyone in there.

Shaking her head, she made her way back around the tiny house.

Inside the bookstore, she took off her coat again and picked up her coffee to take another sip. Looking down, she noticed slushy footprints on the floor.

Lewis's footprints, she thought. *And my own.*

But there were three different sets of footprints.

Someone else had been in the bookstore.

She stared at her cup of coffee, the steam coming off the black liquid.

One word rose in her mind, and it raised the hairs on her neck.

Aconite.

CHAPTER 30

*T*hat evening at the What the Dickens Diner, Alice, Becca, and Ona ate a delicious meal together: Becca's sauerkraut stew with sausages. It was good wintry food that filled Alice to the brim, and afterward, she felt she could've gone straight to sleep.

But she was waiting for a special guest. Besides, Becca and Ona wanted to go back over what had happened. Who could've made that thumping sound to distract her and then poison her coffee? Well, the killer, of course. But who was the killer?

"My money's on Kendra," Ona said.

"Kendra Digby?" Becca said, shocked. "But why would she kill Wade?"

Ona couldn't answer that. Nor could Alice. They'd gone back over this again and again.

When they were drinking decaf coffee and nibbling cookies, the special guest arrived. It was Lenny Stout, the county coroner. He flew in the door, the wind and snow whipping around him.

He hurried to their booth, shook off the snow, and sat

BLACK

down. His clothes were in disarray, as if he'd been tossed about by a hurricane. But then he always looked that way.

"You were right, of course," he said, as Becca served him a cup of warm coffee. "There was aconite in your coffee. Enough to kill an elephant."

The four of them sat in silence for a while. Becca reached across the table and took Alice's hand and squeezed it. She didn't need to say anything. Alice understood. Her death would've devastated her friends.

But I'm not dead. The killer didn't get me.

"The killer's worried," she said. "The distraction—trying to frame Vickers—failed. And something we did recently has unnerved the killer even more."

"But what?" Ona asked.

Alice thought she knew. "My visit to the Digbys. That must be it. I got a little too close for comfort."

"You think Abigail Digby killed Wade?"

Alice considered it. "Mariella Ridgeway said she had solid grounds for divorce because Wade was having an affair. She'd spotted him sitting in a car with Abigail Digby. He'd also called her on his cell phone. But Mariella must've been mistaken. Abigail wasn't having an affair with Wade. They met because he was blackmailing her. But what secret of hers would be blackmail worthy?" She thought long and hard. "What's the worst thing that could happen to Abigail?"

"That's easy," Ona said. "A divorce in which she lost out on much of her husband's money. Maybe Wade wanted more money than she could pay and he was going to talk. That's a powerful motive for Abigail to kill him."

"True. But does Abigail have access to aconite? I don't think so."

"Her daughter does."

"Sure, but Abigail and her daughter aren't on great terms

—they don't even live in the same wing of the big mansion. They—"

Alice stopped herself.

That was it. Kendra lived in the east wing. Yet Ben's scarf was found in Abigail's living room.

"Kendra and Ben," she muttered to herself. "Ben and Abigail."

"What?" Becca asked. "You're not making sense."

"Actually, it all makes sense now."

Then she remembered the damaged elf float, and Mohammad struggling to fix it. But it was the reindeer's head that came loose in the wind and clobbered her.

She got to her feet.

"We need to go to the Christmas fair," she said. "Right away."

Desperate now, the killer would try to remove the evidence to cover his tracks. They'd have to move fast.

Becca and Ona got up. Lenny stayed where he was, warming his hands on the coffee cup. "If there are any dead bodies," he said, "call me."

The three friends hurried down Main Street, tugging their coats around their necks and fighting against the wind. It gusted at them, shoving them. Alice gritted her teeth against the cold and plowed ahead.

Please, don't let us be too late...

At the Pemberley Inn, she led her friends through the little parking lot. The gate to the back stood open. An archway, newly erected over it, said, "Welcome to the Blithedale Christmas Fair."

They entered the grounds. The tiny houses were dark. But here and there, staff from Ridgeway Cleaning still carried boxes to the miniature houses or ensured electrical cables were fastened and covered to meet regulations.

Alice made a beeline for the back.

155

"Where are we going?" Ona called out.

"The floats," Alice said and pointed ahead to where the parade floats stood clustered together.

On the way, she collided with a man.

He grabbed her by the shoulders to stop her.

"Miss Hartford," he said, as startled as she was.

"Please, call me Alice." She smiled. "You're exactly the person I was looking for."

"I am?"

She pointed to the floats. "I want to take a look at the floats. I'm curious—did you fix Rudolph?"

Mohammad frowned. "I tried. Both the elf and the reindeer keep coming undone. The elf was damaged when it arrived, but the reindeer…" He shook his head. "I don't know what happened to the reindeer. Maybe it was ready to break."

Alice doubted that. But she didn't say so. Instead, she asked a question: "What's inside?"

"Inside Rudolph? Nothing. It's hollow."

"I thought so. Do you have a ladder we can borrow?"

Mohammad pointed to a ladder leaning against the nearby porta-potties.

"But why, Miss Hartford? What's going on?" he asked.

"Come and I'll show you."

She hurried over to the ladder and grabbed one end. Ona grabbed the other.

Together, they carried it to the Rudolph float and raised it. While Ona and Becca steadied the ladder, Alice clambered up, the wind buffeting her. It tore at her and shook her, but with one firm grip at a time, she made it to the reindeer's head.

At the top, she studied the seam running along Rudolph's neck. She could see the work Mohammad had done to seal it. The wire was already coming loose, though.

"I'm sorry, Mohammad. I have to do this."

"Miss Hartford—uh, Alice. What are you doing?"

She grabbed the wire and tore at it. It came loose. The wind rippled the float's material, greedily tearing at it. It helped Alice's efforts and shook the wire free. Soon the reindeer's head opened up as the wind tried to lift it off its body.

She had to raise her voice to be heard over the wind. "The original stitching was strong. At first, it held in the wind. Unlike the elf, which was faulty. That one came loose. But then the reindeer did, too. Why? Not because of the wind. But because someone had taken out the original stitching and replaced it, using the same kind of wire you were using for repairs, Mohammad."

She pushed the reindeer's head back. Then reached into the hollow space and rooted around. It was hollow and—my God, what if she was wrong?—seemed empty.

Then she felt something. Something attached to the inside. She tore at it. It took a few tries, but then there was the tearing of tape and it came free.

She brought it out of its hiding place.

It was a leather pouch.

She hugged it to her chest and climbed down to the ground.

Becca, Ona, and Mohammad gathered around as Alice undid the brass snap and lifted the flap. Inside were dozens of papers and photographs. Careful not to let the wind tear them out of her hands, she shuffled through them and brought out a photo.

It was a blurry photograph. Apparently taken with a long lens at some distance, it had captured a scene through a window. Alice recognized the sofas and armchairs and the big glass coffee table. Abigail Digby straddled a man on the sofa. She was buck naked—apart from one item of clothing: a red scarf.

Another photograph had caught the man dressing. Again,

it was blurry, so his face wasn't identifiable. He was wrapping the scarf around his neck as Abigail, also blurry, wrapped her arms around him.

Mohammad muttered something in Arabic. Then said, "That must be Mr. Ridgeway—I mean, Ben."

"With Abigail Digby," Alice said, confirming the guess. "And this is what Wade was using to blackmail her. It would've been grounds for divorce. She might've lost a great deal of the wealth she enjoyed. And it's why Ben—"

A man cleared his throat.

"That's right—it's why I confronted him."

Ben Ridgeway stood a few paces from them, his hands in the pockets of his winter coat, a blue scarf wrapped around his neck. His face looked like a specter of his former self—his eyes sunk into dark hollows, his skin both pale and blotchy.

"You discovered your dad was blackmailing your lover," Alice said.

"Abigail told me, of course. She couldn't keep it a secret from me. So I told Dad to back off. He laughed." Ben winced, as if the memory was physically painful. "He laughed about me and Abigail. He was cruel. Always had been. For years, I'd hated him, but that day, I hated him so much that I almost strangled him. He mocked me. He said he thought I was in love with Kendra." Ben snorted. "Kendra. That hippie-dippy girl is nothing like her mother. Abigail Digby is like a movie star from the 1950s. She's stylish. She's classy. And she's mine."

Alice said, "But she isn't, Ben. She's Clyde Digby's wife."

Ben frowned. "She's working that out. She's entitled to her fair share. Once she figures out how to divorce Digby and keep what she wants, we're going to elope."

The crazed look in his eyes disturbed her. He looked like he hadn't slept for days. And he spoke as if his plans with Abigail would still work out.

Alice said, "You know, Ben, that doesn't sound like a fifty-fifty divorce settlement. Maybe you're expecting too much..."

"Abigail deserves everything she's got," he snapped. "And Dad would've taken it from her."

"So you poisoned him."

As the wind howled around him, Ben smiled, almost wistfully. "It was a good plan. I knew about Kendra's herbal remedies. So I made up a sob story about anxiety and she made a special anti-anxiety tea for me. It contained aconite." His smiled broadened at the mention of the poison. "I was close to her. I'd used our friendship as an excuse to visit Abigail. Well, I got even closer, indulging in Kendra's fantasy that we might be more than friends, and it gave me access to her store of aconite. The rest was easy. I put the poison in my dad's cup, and when he was dead, I grabbed the leather pouch." His mouth quirked. "But the fair was crawling with people. The leather pouch stood out. What if people realized it was my dad's? I needed to hide it. I'd been helping Mohammad with the floats. I opened Rudolph's head and then sealed it again. Unfortunately, the damn thing wouldn't stay closed, and every time I returned to get the damn thing, I bumped into people. I was worried they would see me with the pouch."

"You came tonight to remove the evidence once and for all."

"I was waiting for people to leave." He gazed around at the tiny house village. "But my colleagues are still working. I didn't want to risk it." He sighed. "Now I have to risk everything."

He pulled his hands out of his pockets. In his right hand, he held a gun. The wind buffeted him.

"I'll do anything for Abigail. She's a goddess. She's the love of my life." His voice cracked with emotion as he yelled to be heard over the wind. "Now, give me the evidence, and no one gets hurt."

He's gone crazy, Alice thought. *Even without the evidence, he's confessed to four witnesses that he killed his father.*

But she didn't tell Ben that. She held out the leather pouch and took a step forward, offering it to him. He snatched it from her.

Pressing it against his stomach, he backed away, the gun still aimed at Alice.

The wind whipped through the fairgrounds. A snap and an ear-rending *riiiiiiiip* made him look up. It made them all gaze up at the floats. The wind had finally won its battle, tearing Rudolph's head off. It flew off the reindeer's body and landed between Alice and Ben with a thump.

Pushed by the wind, it slid across the ground.

Alice stuck out a boot and brought it down on the edge of the neck, pinning it down. Meanwhile, Ben turned on his heels and bolted. Which was what she'd expected. He ran toward the exit.

Downwind, she thought. *Perfect.*

She crouched down and grabbed the reindeer's head and lifted it with all her strength and threw it. It sailed through the air, lifting momentarily as air streamed under it, but then the wind smacked it down.

"Bull's eye!" Ona shouted as the reindeer head landed on Ben.

One moment Ben was running, the next he was wearing a massive Rudolph's head. He staggered to the side, arms flailing, and collided with a tiny house. The impact made a loud thump, like the one he'd made when he'd thrown himself against Wonderland Books to draw Alice outside.

The collision must've frightened him, because he raised the gun and fired. Alice ducked. But the bullet went off into the air, vanishing into the night, and startling Ben. He dropped the gun, and teetered backward, tripped, and toppled to the ground.

Both hands free, he now used them to wrestle the reindeer head off.

In a flash, Ona reached Ben, followed closely by Becca and Mohammad, and the three of them held Ben down to the ground. He continued to struggle.

"Let me out! Let me out of this damn thing!"

Alice kicked the gun away from him. He'd dropped the leather pouch, too. She picked it up and gripped it firmly as she heard sirens in the distance.

If Ben hadn't threatened to kill them, the scene would've been laugh-out-loud funny. A man with a giant reindeer head kicked and wriggled on the ground, held down by three people as he cried out, "Get this reindeer off me!"

Alice smiled, letting out a breath.

It was over. And just in time for Christmas, too.

CHAPTER 31

*D*uring the night, the wind calmed down, and by the time the Christmas fair opened the next morning, the skies were blue, festooned with fluffy white clouds. The smell of coffee and cookies wafted across the tiny house village as people streamed into the reopened fair.

At the center of the tiny house village stood a massive Christmas tree, decorated with huge glass balls, thick tinsel, and a rich variety of other ornaments. Lights festooned the branches. A star topped the tree.

"It's perfect," Alice gushed when she saw it.

"And it came just in the nick of time," Becca said.

"Saint Nick of time?" Ona suggested with a wink.

They'd gathered in front of the small stage, along with everyone else at the fair. On stage stood Mayor MacDonald. He was substituting for Abigail Digby, who had called in sick, and for Vickers, who was in custody for fraud and selling counterfeit goods. Bunce, who'd agreed to pay back the Santa prize from last year, got more lenient treatment, and was headed back to Florida. The mayor held an envelope in which was the name of the best Santa of the year.

"It's with great pleasure that I announce this year's winner of the Santa Claus contest."

He smiled at the audience.

"And our Santa is…"

The audience held its breath.

"…Clyde Digby!"

Clyde Digby, wearing a Santa costume, walked on stage and the crowd roared and clapped. He waved at them, smiling. Then took the microphone.

"I'm honored you've voted for me. Even though I wasn't on the ballot." He chuckled. "But I tell you what, I did this whole secret Santa thing to spark more joy of reading. Not to compete in a contest. So that's what the prize money will go toward. I'm donating—and doubling—the full amount to a charity to ensure kids in under-resourced communities get the books they need. How about that?"

The audience erupted into loud applause and someone began singing, "For he's a jolly good fellow," as Clyde walked off stage.

Mr. and Mrs. Oriel stood near Alice and her friends, and Mrs. Oriel turned to them and said, "That man is a real Santa."

"And a good writer, too," Mr. Oriel said.

His wife nudged him and gave him a suggestive wink.

The Pointed Firs walked on stage and after tuning up their instruments—banjo, bass, fiddle, and guitar—they launched into a bluegrass rendition of "Rudolph the Red-Nosed Reindeer." Althea, the lead singer, caught Alice's eye and winked at her.

Alice laughed. "You told Althea about our adventures last night?" she asked Ona.

"Didn't have to. Did you see *The Blithedale Record* this morning? Every article was marked 'breaking news.' Todd's got an exclusive interview with you, a full report on the murder of Wade Ridgeway, and a heartwarming tale of a secret, book-loving Santa, who happens to be a bestselling romance novelist."

Becca chuckled. "Todd's in seventh heaven."

But outside Bonsai & Pie, Alice saw someone who wasn't in seventh heaven. Mariella and Kendra sat huddled together under a patio heater, drinking coffee and talking in low voices. Their eyes looked sunken and red. No doubt neither had slept much during the night. Their wounds would take a long time to heal—Mariella had lost her son to prison while Kendra's heart was broken. She'd been betrayed by both her mother and the man she loved. But maybe this would bring the two of them together, and that would be a silver lining.

Alice realized it was the first time she'd seen Mariella sit still.

But another person in a blue Ridgeway Cleaning jacket was hurrying across the fairgrounds, stopping to talk to Mohammad. It was Lewis Tuttle. Mariella had offered him a job, glad to hire a hard-working guy with business experience, especially now that her son, her second-in-command, was gone.

Mohammad, who had filled Alice in on Lewis's improved luck, had also shared that the two of them were working together to manage the fair, so Mrs. Ridgeway—"Mariella," he corrected himself—could take some time off.

Across the fairgrounds, Mohammad and Lewis gathered alongside others to prepare for the parade, hitching horses to the carriages that would pull the floats.

Among them, Alice noticed Chief Jimbo. Today, he wore no uniform. State police patrolled the fair. He'd handed over the responsibility to Captain Burlap's colleagues and told Mayor MacDonald he was going on sick leave to—in his own words—"figure out what's next."

"He looks healthier and happier than I've ever seen him," Alice said, gesturing toward the crowd of people by the floats.

"Who?" Ona said. "Jimbo? Yeah, maybe he's finally taking charge of his own life."

"Good for him," Becca said.

They watched the volunteers position the repaired Rudolph float at the front, lining the other horse-drawn floats behind it. Visitors noticed and word began to spread through the crowds of people milling around the stalls, and some began to line up by the parade route through the tiny village town.

"So many people," Alice remarked.

Ona grinned. "We're a hit."

She was right. Despite the murder investigation, the fair had turned out to be a hit, bringing in more people than expected—they could put aside their concerns about Blithedale going bankrupt. And it wasn't over yet.

"The grand finale's about to begin," Becca said. "But there's still time for coffee and something sweet, right?"

They all agreed. Heading into Bonsai & Pie's tiny house, Alice, Becca, and Ona ogled the display case full of pies. Alice noticed a gift-wrapped package on the counter, but thought little of it.

All three of them ordered slices of eggnog pie. As they sat by the counter, eating pie and drinking coffee, Alice said, "You know, I didn't think I would like eggnog pie. But this is delicious."

"Andrea's pies never disappoint," Ona said, and from behind the counter, Andrea blew her a kiss.

"Like Christmas in Blithedale," Becca said. "Every year, it's even sweeter than I remembered."

It wasn't until someone called out, "The parade is starting," that they finished the last bits of crust on their plates. Before heading out, Alice raised her coffee cup, and the three friends made a toast to the holidays. "And a Merry Christmas to all."

Alice was following Becca and Ona outside when Andrea called her name.

"Don't forget your present."

"What present?"

Andrea pointed to the gift-wrapped package sitting on the counter.

"That's not mine," Alice said, but when she picked it up, she saw the label had her name on it.

"For Alice," it said. "Thank you." Nothing else.

She tore the wrapping paper off, and knew at once who'd left a present for her.

Inside was a book. Warmth spread through her chest—like the feeling of coming home—when she recognized the cover. It was one of her childhood favorites: *The Hidden Staircase*. And it was, of course, the second book in the Nancy Drew Mystery Stories series.

She'd been meaning to reread it for years. This Christmas she would. And she'd make sure to buy herself book one, too.

* * *

Thank you so much for visiting Blithedale.

Want a free short story? Sign up for my newsletter to hear when the next Wonderland Books Cozy Mystery comes out and I'll send the free cozy mystery story to you by email:

https://mpblackbooks.com/newsletter/

Finally, if you enjoyed this book, please take a moment to leave a review online. It makes it easier for other readers to find the book. Thanks so much!

Turn the page to see what other books are available.

MORE BY M.P. BLACK

A Wonderland Books Cozy Mystery Series

A Bookshop to Die For

A Theater to Die For

A Halloween to Die For

A Christmas to Die For

An Italian-American Cozy Mystery Series

The Soggy Cannoli Murder

Sambuca, Secrets, and Murder

Tastes Like Murder

Meatballs, Mafia, and Murder

Short stories

The Italian Cream Cake Murder

ABOUT THE AUTHOR

M.P. Black writes fun cozies with an emphasis on food, books, and travel — and, of course, a good old murder mystery.

In addition to writing and publishing his own books, he helps others fulfill their author dreams too.

M.P. Black has lived in many places, including Austria, Costa Rica, and the United Kingdom. Today, he lives in Copenhagen, Denmark, with his family.

Join M.P. Black's free newsletter for updates on books and special deals:

https://mpblackbooks.com/newsletter/

Made in the USA
Las Vegas, NV
21 May 2024

90210998R00104